James Hamilton

The Happy Home

affectionately inscribed to the working people

James Hamilton

The Happy Home
affectionately inscribed to the working people

ISBN/EAN: 9783337406301

Printed in Europe, USA, Canada, Australia, Japan

Cover: Foto ©Andreas Hilbeck / pixelio.de

More available books at **www.hansebooks.com**

FRONTISPIECE.

Happy Home.

THE HAPPY HOME.

By Rev. James Hamilton.

THE

HAPPY HOME:

AFFECTIONATELY INSCRIBED TO

THE WORKING PEOPLE.

BY THE

REV. JAMES HAMILTON, D. D.,

AUTHOR OF "LIFE IN EARNEST," "HARP ON THE WILLOWS,"
"MOUNT OF OLIVES," "THANKFULNESS," "LIFE OF HALL," ETC.

With Illustrations by Howland

CONTENTS.

PREFACE.

THE writer of the following pages has some acquaintance with working-men. In early life he numbered many of them among his friends — was admitted to their meetings for religious and intellectual improvement — and at the table of a noble-minded relative, who regarded piety as the true gentility, he met them as frequent guests. Subsequent years have given him no reason to regret that intercourse, nor to repudiate those ancient friendships; but they have taught him that British Christianity is ill acquainted with British industry. Seldom, for instance, has he found a religious book entirely suited to the laborer as he is. We have good books in abundance, but they are usually written with an eye to the parlor or boudoir. And we have myriads of tracts; but their topics and their style are mostly a tradition from Hannah More, and do not meet our modern exi-

1*

gency. "Sorrowful Sam" and "Diligent Dick" are gone the way of all living, and a new generation has started up: a generation shrewd, active, and knowing; a generation of vigorous minds, fond of information, and bent on improvement. To that generation these papers are inscribed. Their author writes for the English and Scottish operative, for the mechanic, the daily laborer, and the artisan. He does not constitute himself their patron or their censor; he will be content if he can earn the name of friend. And with a view to this, he will tell the truths which he deems most urgent; and tell them simply, as they are simple to his own perception — and briefly, for they are busy men whose leisure he solicits.

With politics he does not intermeddle. From his faith in Christianity, he has great hope for the popular future; but, anxious to secure a tranquil hearing for matters more urgent, he abstains from subjects of ephemeral interest. He has too much love for the gospel to employ it as gilding for party-prescriptions, and too much reverence for the Bible to use it as a bird-lime for the politicians who fly, or a ground-bait for those who grovel. So far as it is known to himself, his aim is philanthropic, and he asks no help from any civil faction. Nor is he recruiting for a religious sect. He has his favorite haunts, and it is long since he fixed his denominational dwelling. But

Kent need not contend with Cornwall, because
the one fends off the sea with cliffs of chalk, and
the other with granite bulwarks; or because the
one gleans its wealth on the surface, and the other
digs it from the depths. Each is a portion of the
same favored isle, and each helps to make the
other rich. And, blessed be God! there is such a
thing as evangelic patriotism. The writer seeks
the extension of the universal church. His creed
is the gospel; his sect is Christianity; and "One
is his Master, even Jesus Christ."

His mission is to working-men. He knows
that few of them are happy. Some of them subscribe to the sentiment of a popular Frenchman:
"The Redeemer has come; the redemption is not
come yet." They forget that it was to the world
that the Redeemer came, and that it is to the individual that the redemption comes. To render
evident this truth is the object of the following
pages; and in the attempt we shall take for
guides those famous working-men who once rev-
olutionized the world, and who infected many a
gloomy spirit with their own exuberant blessedness. Listening to their lesson, we learn that
God has made every man the keeper of his own
comfort. We find that happiness is not a political adjustment, but a personal possession. We
are told that, however wrong the state of society,
the religion of Jesus is portable and self-contained

felicity.   We shall go back to the times of these
tent-makers, and sit beside them as they shape
the canvass and carve the stretching-pins,* and
will ask them why they sing those stately psalms,
and feel so rich amid their poverty. And whether read in an English cottage or on a colonial
wild, by the village laborer or the city artisan,
we trust and pray that the answer may reveal to
some who have not found it yet — the secret of a
HAPPY HOME.

SATURDAY, *June* 17, 1848.

* Acts xviii. 3

PETER THE GREAT.

HAPPY HOME

THE FRIEND OF THE PEOPLE.

LAST century a Russian emperor gained much renown by the exertions and sacrifices he made for his dominions. Impressed by their savage state, and eager to introduce the arts and accomplishments of more cultured nations, he resolved to become himself the engineer and preceptor of his people. Instead of sending a few clever men to glean what they could in foreign regions, he determined to be his own envoy; and leaving his Moscow palace, he set out to travel in Holland and Great Britain. He was particularly anxious to carry home the art of naval architecture; for he wisely judged, that without ships and seamen, his empire would never be able to turn its own resources to account. However, he soon found that no man could learn to be a ship-builder by merely looking on; but whatever it might need, Peter was determined to do. With a noble energy, he changed his gay clothing for the garb of a carpenter, and spent week after week in the building-yard at Saardam, wielding the hatchet, flourishing the tar-brush, and driving bolts till the pent-house rang again; and soon was he able to go home and teach his people how to build ships for themselves. No wonder that, while other monarchs are depicted in purple and ermine, the artist should prefer representing Peter, the czar of Muscovy, in his red woollen jacket, and crowned with the glazed hat of a sailor, with a timber log for his throne, and an adze for his sceptre. And no wonder that a grateful country should rear to his memory the proudest column in the world, and christen by his name its capital.

Far nobler than this achievement of the emperor Peter, are some facts recorded in the history of philanthropy. It was a nobler thing, for instance, when, in order to gain personal knowledge of its horrors, and to be able to testify against them afterward, an English gentleman took his passage in an African slaver, and submitted voluntarily to months of filth and fever, at the peril of his life, and to the hourly torture of his feelings. And still nobler was the conduct of those angelic missionaries, who, finding no other way to introduce the gospel among the negroes of Barbadoes, sold themselves to slavery, and then told their fellow-bondsmen the news which sets the spirit free. And noblest of all was the self-devotion of two Moravians, of whom some of you have read. They were filled with pity for the inmates of a fearful lazaretto. It was an enclosure in which persons afflicted with leprosy were confined; and so terrified for

its contagion were the people, that once
within the dismal gates, no one was suffered
to quit them again. But the state of its
doomed inmates so preyed on these compassionate men, that they resolved at all
hazard to cheer them in captivity, and to
try to save their souls. They counted the
cost. They said: " Farewell, freedom —
farewell, society — farewell, happy sun and
healthy breezes ;" and passed the return-
less portals, each a living sacrifice.

The state of our world touched with
compassion the Son of God. He left his
home in heaven, and came hither. The
King of kings put off his glory. He came
to this scene of guilt and misery. He left
the adoring fellowship above, and came
down among creatures who disliked him,
and could not comprehend him. On his
benevolent errand, he alighted on this
plague-stricken planet, and became for
more than thirty years identified with its
inmates, and in perpetual contact with its
sin and its sorrow. And while his eye was

intent on some bright consummation, he did not grudge to be for many years the exile and prisoner, and at last the victim.

And I think it should be interesting to you, to remember the lot in human life which the Saviour selected. He had his choice. He might have chosen for his residence a mansion or a palace; but he chose for his domicil, so long as he had one, the cottage of a carpenter. He cast his earthly lot alongside of the laboring man; and besides the intentional lowlihood, there were other ends it answered.

It lent new dignity to labor. Some silly people feel it a disgrace to work; they blush to be detected in an act of industry. They fancy that it is dignity to have nothing to do, and a token of refinement to be able to do nothing. They forget that it is easy to be useless, and that it needs no talent to cumber the ground. But the Lord Jesus knew that it is best for the world when all are workers; and he conformed to the good rule of Palestine, which required every cit-

izen to pursue some employment. And
instead of selecting a brilliant occupation,
he gave himself to one humble and com-
monplace, that we might learn how possible
it is to do extraordinary good in a very
inconspicuous station.

And by this selection he left an example
to working men. Rough work is no reason for rude manners or a vulgar mind.
Never did there traverse the globe a presence so pure, and a fascination so divine,
as moved about in the person of the "carpenter's son." So gentle in his dignity;
so awful in his meekness; so winsome in
his lovingness; so dexterous in diffusing
happiness; so delicate in healing inward
hurts; so gracious in forestalling wishes!
no rules of etiquette, no polish of society,
can ever yield anew the same majestic
suavity. Amid the daily drudgery, his
soul was often swelling with its wondrous
purpose; and while shaping for the boors
of Galilee their implements of industry, his
spirit was commercing with the sky. They

are not little occupations, but little thoughts
and little notions, which make the little
man; and the grandeur of mien, and the
engaging manners, which emerged from
that Nazarene workshop, are a lesson to
those who handle the hammer, the spade,
or the shuttle. But far more,—the sanctity. In a town of bad repute—forced
into the company of ruffians and blasphemers,—all the uncongenial fellowship
showed him the more conspicuously "holy,
harmless, undefiled, separate from sinners."
And if you complain that you are shut up
to the society of loose and low-minded
men—if constrained to listen to words
ribald and profane, or to witness coarse
debauchery—remember that it was in the
guise of a laboring man that the Saviour
fought the world's corruption, and over-
came. And if like to be worsted, cry for
help to Him who, among his other memories of earth, remembers Galilee;—who,
now that he has done with the carpenter's
shop for ever, has not forgotten the surly

neighbors and the abandoned town; and whose solitary example destroyed the proverb, " Can any good thing come out of Nazareth ?"

And by choosing this humble lot, the Saviour learned to sympathize with penury. Whatever wealthy bards may sing of the sweets of poverty, it is a painful thing to be very poor. To be a poor man's child, and look through the rails of the playground, and envy richer boys for the sake of their many books, and yet be doomed to ignorance ; to be apprenticed to some harsh stranger, and feel for ever banished from a mother's tenderness and a sister's love; to work when very weary ; to work when the heart is sick and the head is sore ; to see a wife or a darling child wasting away, and not be **able** to get the best advice ; to hope that better food or purer air might set her up again, but that food you can not buy — that air you must never hope to breathe ; to be obliged to let her die ; to come home from the daily task, some evening, and see her sinking; to sit up all night, in hope to catch again those precious words you might have heard could you have afforded to stay at home all day, but never hear them; to have no mourners at the funeral, or even carry on your own shoulder through the merry streets the light deal coffin; to see huddled into a promiscuous hole the dust which is so dear to you, and not venture to mark the spot by planted flower or lowliest stone; some bitter winter, or some costly spring, to barter for food the clock or the curious cupboard, or the "Henry's Commentary," on which you prided yourself as the heir-loom of a frugal family, and never be able to redeem it; to feel that you are getting old—nothing laid aside, and present earnings scarce sufficient; to change the parlor floor for the top story, and the top story for a single attic, and wonder what change will be the next;—these and a thousand privations are the pains of poverty. And in the days when the world's Redeemer occupied the poor

2*

man's home, he was familiar with sights the parallels of these. He noted them — he entered into them — he shared them. Even at the time, he did somewhat to relieve them. It was in such a scene that he let forth the first glimpse of his glory. The scanty store of wine had failed at a marriage-feast, and, to relieve the embarrassment of his humble entertainers, he created a new supply. And it was in a similar scene that the second of his healing miracles was wrought, and his entrance to Simon's fishing-hut was signalized by restoring from a fever his sick mother-in-law. And, not to dwell on the miracles of mercy which restored to the widow of Nain her only son, and to the sisters of Bethany their only brother, it is worth while to notice how many of his wonders were presents to the poor. A weary boatman has swept the waves all night and captured not a single fin. Jesus bids him drop the net in a particular spot, and instantly it welters with a silvery spoil.

Again and again the eager throng hangs
round him till the sun is setting, and it is
discovered that there are only a few small
loaves among all the fainting thousands;
but he speaks the word, and as little loaves
bulk out an endless banquet, the famished
villagers rejoice in the rare repast. And
though he did not grudge his cures to cen
turions and rulers of the synagogues, they
were usually the poor and despised who
craved and got the largest share — the
woman who had spent on physicians all that
she had; the impotent man at Bethesda;
the Samaritan lepers; and Bartimeus, the
blind beggar. And thus would the kind
Redeemer teach us, that if there are always
to be the poor on earth, there will always
be the poor man's Friend in heaven. He
would teach those sons of toil who are his
true disciples, that in all their afflictions he
is afflicted; that he knows their frame and
feels their sorrow. And should these lines
be read by one who is indigent in spite of
all his industry, let him remember how it

fared with the world's best benefactor when here below—let him remember that the Saviour himself had once nowhere to lay his head, and asking for a cup of cold water, could scarcely obtain it. But now that he has all power in heaven and earth, that Saviour is as tender as ever; and to you, oh children of want and wo! he says, "Come unto me, all ye that labor and are heavy laden, and I will give you rest."

But I hasten to notice the greatest boon which the Saviour purchased. Returning to an instance already mentioned: had you seen the devoted missionaries pass into the leper hospital, along with admiration of their kindness, you would have felt a grievous pang at such an immolation. To think that men in the height of health should thus be lost to the land of the living—that good men and generous should be buried quick in such a ghastly grave—it would have oppressed your spirit, and you could only have given grudging approbation to such a

self-devotement. But if, at the end of a
certain term, they had appeared at the gate
again, and along with them a goodly band
of the poor victims restored to perfect
soundness; if it turned out that they had
not only been able to mitigate much suffering, but, in the case of every one who submitted to their treatment, had effected a
perfect cure; and if, on examining the
matter, the competent authorities declared
that not only were these heroes of humanity
themselves uninjured, but that those whom
they brought with them were clean every
whit, and might forthwith pass out into the
world of the hale and the happy, you would
be more than reconciled to the great price
which purchased such a wondrous restoration. When Immanuel went into this
world—when he first put human nature
on, and in all his innocence identified him
self with the fate of sinful men—we might
almost imagine the anxiety awakened by
this "mystery of godliness" in any celestial spirit who did not foreknow the issue

But when that issue was developed—when, with a multitude which no man can number, rescued and restored, the mighty Redeemer reappeared at the gate of the lazaretto—when infinite purity, and eterna justice, and the holy law, recognised not only an immaculate Deliverer, but in all his ransomed company could detect no stain of sin, no spot of the old corruption—when it was pronounced that millions of plague-stricken beings were now so convalescent and so pure, that they might even pass the pearly gates and join the fellowship of angels, enough was seen to justify the self-denial, though that self-denial was the incarnation of the Son of God—enough to recompense the sacrifice, though that sacrifice was the death of a Divine Redeemer.

But this was the simple fact : An Angel of mercy, a Volunteer of pure compassion, the Saviour assumed our nature, and visited our world. The Word was made flesh, and dwelt among us. And, coming

into the world, he came into a moral lazaretto. Young and old, rich and poor,
every soul was smitten with sin's disgusting
malady. None were holy; none sought
after God. All were corrupt; all were, to
God's pure eye, offensive; and all were
sickening toward the second death. And
by coming hither and taking on the human
nature, the Son of God committed himself
to our woful case. He virtually declared,
that unless he brought a convalescent company with him, he would return to heaven
no more. But the balsam which alone
could heal this malady, was found to be
very costly. It must contain, as an ingre-
dient, something which could compensate
for sin; something so compensating, that
God would be a just God in forgiving the
sinner. And nothing, it was found, could
atone for guilt, save blood divine. But
Jesus had counted the cost; and even this
price he was prepared to pay. And he
paid it: he offered himself as the propitiation for sin, and he was accepted. And

though among those whom he sought to save were atheists and infidels, murderers and liars, blasphemers and sabbath-breakers, thieves and robbers, drunkards and debauchees, that one offering was infinite, and more than sufficed. It finished transgression, and the Supreme Judge and Lawgiver proclaimed it to the world, " The blood of Jesus Christ cleanseth from all sin." And reappearing at the gates of Paradise with his ransomed, " the gates lifted up their heads ;" and having long since returned from that errand of kindness, and rejoined the acclaiming celestials, already has the King of Glory been followed by many a trophy of his life-giving death and peace-speaking blood. Dear reader, will not you be another? Will you not intrust your soul to One so skilful to heal, and so mighty to save? Will you not begin to sing that new song even here, " Thou art worthy; for thou wast slain, and hast redeemed us to God by thy blood ?" And will you not, from this time forward, give a higher place in your affections to that adorable Friend, " who, though he was rich, for your sakes became poor, that ye through his poverty might be rich?"

3

THE man was very poor, and one of those poor men who never make it any better. Always so laggard and so listless, he looked as if he had come into the world with only half his soul. Having no fondness for exertion, he had great faith in windfalls; and once or twice he was favored with a windfall; but as he took no pains to secure it and turn it to account, the same fickle element which brought it soon wafted it away. His character was gone; his principles, never firm, were fast decaying; and between laziness and bad habits, he was little better than the ruin of a man. He had a brother far away; but so many years had come and gone since last he was seen in those regions, that he was faintly recollected. Indeed, so long since was it, that this

THE DISCONSOLATE MAN.

Happy Home.   p 27

man had no remembrance of him. But one evening a messenger came to him, telling him that his brother lived, and in token of his love, had sent him the present of a gallant ship with all its cargo. The man was in a heartless mood. He was sitting in his dingy chamber; no fire on the hearth, no loaf in the cupboard, no pence in his pocket, no credit in that neighborhood, bleak weather in the world, bleak feelings in his soul. And as, with folded arms, he perched on an empty chest and listened to the news, he neither wondered nor rejoiced. Sure enough it was a windfall; but he was not just then in a romantic or wistful mood, and so he heard it sullenly. No; he neither danced nor capered, neither laughed nor shouted, but coldly walked away — scarcely hoping, scarcely caring to find it true. And when, at last, he reached the port, and espied the ship, it dispelled all his boyish dreams of eastern merchantmen. The masts were not palms, with silken cords furling the purple sails; nor did its bulwarks gild the

water, and its beams of sandal scent the
air. It was much like the barques around
it—chafed, and weathered, and bleached by
the billows, and bore no outward token of a
gorgeous freight. But stepping on board,
as soon as the master of the vessel knew
who he was, he addressed him respectfully,
and descanted with glowing warmth on the
glories and generosity of his absent brother,
and then invited him below to feast his eyes
on his new possession. There was gold,
and the red ingots looked so rich, and
weighed in the hand so heavy; there were
robes, stiff with embroidery, and bright
with ruby and sapphire stars; there were
spices such as the fervid sun distils from
the fragrant soil in that exuberant zone, and
dainties such as only load the tropic trees.
Nor in the wealthy invoice had forethought
and affection omitted any good; for there
were even some herbs and anodynes of
singular power; a balm which healed en-
venomed wounds; an ointment which
brought back the failing sight; a cordial

which kept from fainting; and a preparation which made the wearer proof against the fire. And there was a bulky parchment, the title-deeds to a large domain somewhere in that sunny land; and along with all a letter, distinct and full, in the princely donor's autograph. Of that letter, the younger brother sat down and read a portion there; and as he read, he looked around him to see that it was all reality; and then he read again, and his lip quivered, and his eye filled, and as the letter dropped upon his lap, he smote upon his breast, and called himself by some bitter name. And then he started up; and if you had only seen him — such an altered man; such energy, and yet such mildness; such affection, and withal such heroism as beamed of a sudden in his kindling countenance; you would have thought that, amid its other wonders, that foreign ship had fetched the remainder of his soul. And so it had. From that day forward he was another man; grudging no labor, doing nothing by halves, his character changed, his reputation retrieved, his whole existence filled with a new consciousness, and inspired by a new motive, and all his sanguine schemes and cheerful efforts converging toward the happy day which should transport him to the arms of that unseen brother.

Reader, have you lost heart about yourself? Once on a time you had some anxiety about character. You wished that you had greater strength of principle, and that your moral standing were more respectable. You envied the virtuous energy of those friends who can resist temptation, and combat successfully the evil influences around them. You have even wished that you could wake up some morning and find yourself a Christian; and you have sometimes hoped that this happiness might at length befall you. But there is, as yet, no sign of it. Startling providences have passed over you, but they have not frightened you out of your evil habits; and, from time to time, amiable and engaging

friends have gained ascendency over you,
but they have not been able to allure you
into the paths of piety. And now you are
discouraged. You know that some vicious
habit is getting a firmer and more fearful
hold of you, and if you durst own it to
yourself, you have now no hope of a lofty
or virtuous future. You feel abject, and
spiritless, and self-disgusted, and have
nearly made up your mind to saunter slip-
shod down the road to ruin.

You do not remember your Elder
Brother, for he had left those regions before you were born. But this comes to
tell you that he lives and wishes you well.
In the far country whither he has gone, he
knows how you are, and is much concerned
at your present condition. And he feels
for you none the less, that in all that land
he is himself the richest and the mightiest.
And to show that, amid all his glory, he is
not ashamed to be called your brother, he
has sent you a noble gift—a ship freighted
with some of his choicest acquisitions, and

bringing everything good for a man like
you.

And be not vexed nor angry when I tell
you, that that ship of heaven is THE BIBLE.
If, instead of touching at every land and
coming to every door—if only a few Bibles
arrived now and then ready-made and
direct from heaven, and each addressed to
some particular person—and if none besides were allowed to handle their contents
or appropriate their treasures—how justly
might the world envy that favored few!
But having purchased gifts for men while
here among us, and being highly exalted
where he is gone, the Saviour in his kindness sends this heaven-laden book, this
celestial argosie, to all his brethren here
below, and each alike is welcome to its
costly freight. Despise it not! There is
nothing dazzling in its exterior. It is plain
and unpretending. No rainbow lights its
margin, nor do phosphorescent letters come
and go on its azure pages. But the wealth
of the Indian carack is neither its timbers

nor its rigging; it hides its treasure in the
hold. The wonder of the Bible is neither
its binding nor its type—nay, not even
(though these are wonderful) its language
and its style. It makes God glorious, and
the reader blessed, by the wealth it carries
and the truths it tells.

To recite at full the letter, would take
too long. A brother's heart yearns in it
all; but what a holy, and what an exalted
brother! He informs you that all power is
given him in heaven and earth, and that
from his Father he has received such ample
authority, that all throughout these dominions, life and death are in his hands. He
says that he is grieved to know your
wretched position; but he bids you not to
lose heart, for if you only take advantage
of what he has sent you, there will be an
end of your misery. And he adds, that,
freely and lovingly as he forwards these
gifts, they cost him much; they have cost
him labor and sorrow, groans and anguish,
ears and blood. He begs that you will take

frankly what is given kindly, and assures
you that nothing will gladden him more
than to hail you to his home and instal you
in his kingdom. And lest there be any
matter which you do not rightly understand, and on which you would like fuller
information, or more help till then, there is
a very wise and much-loved friend of his,
who is willing to come and abide with you
until he and you shall meet again.

But, begging you to read the letter at
your leisure, let us step for a few minutes
on board. Let us glance at some of those
costly gifts which the Saviour purchased
long ago, and which, in this Book of
Heaven, he sends to our island-planet, and
to the several abodes of us sinners who
inhabit it.

And, first of all, look at this fine GOLD.
Among material substances, the one most
prized is gold. Not only is it very beautiful, but it is the means of procuring each
rare commodity. Hence, we call him a
rich man who abounds in it, and him a

poor man who has got none of it. And in the spiritual domain, the equivalent of gold is goodness. By holy beings, and by God himself, the thing most prized is not money, but moral worth; not gold, but goodness. And when God first ushered on existence his new creature, man, he gave him a portion of heaven's capital to begin with: he gave him holy tastes and dispositions, a pure and pious mind. But man soon lost it. He suffered himself to be defrauded of his original righteousness; and on that dismal day, he who rose the heir of immortality, lay down a bankrupt and a pauper. All was lost; and though he tried to replace it by a glittering counterfeit, the substitute had not one atom of what is essential to genuine goodness. It entirely lacked THE LOVE OF GOD; and no sooner had Jehovah applied the touchstone, than in grief and displeasure he exclaimed, "How is the gold become dim! how is the most fine gold changed!" And yet that gold was essential—nothing could

compensate for it. No merit, then no reward; no righteousness, no heaven And
which guarantied a glorious immortality.
man had lost the only thing which entitled
him to the favor of God—the only thing
It was then that his case was undertaken
by a Kinsman-Redeemer. To a holy humanity he superadded the wisdom and
strength of Deity; and divinely authorized,
he took the field—the surety and representative of ruined man. In his heart he
hid the holy law; and in his sublime fulfil-
ment of it, he magnified that law and made
it honorable. And between the precious
blood he shed, as an expiation for sin, and
the spotless obedience which he offered on
behalf of his people, he wrought out a
redundant and everlasting righteousness.
It was tested, and was found to be without
one particle of alloy. It was put into the
balance, but the sin has never yet been
found which could outweigh the merits of
Immanuel. The righteousness of Christ,
as the sinner's representative, is the most

golden thing in all the gospel; and it is because of its conveying and revealing that righteousness, that the gospel is the power of God, and the wisdom of God unto salvation.* Be counselled to buy this fine gold, and you will be rich.† Accept, poor sinner, this righteousness of the Saviour, and you will be justified freely by a gracious God, through the redemption that is in Christ.‡ God will be well pleased with you because you are well pleased with his beloved Son; and will count you righteous for the sake of that righteousness which the Saviour wrought out, and which the gospel reveals, and which, thankfully receiving, you present to a righteous God as your plea for pardon, and your passport to the kingdom of heaven.

This is the glory of the gospel. IT REVEALS A RIGHTEOUSNESS. And just as the man whose affairs are all entangled would be thankful for money sufficient to discharge his debts, and set him on a foot-

* Rom. i. 16, 17. † Rev. iii. 18. ‡ Rom. iii. 20–26.

ing with his honest neighbors, so the man
who knows himself a debtor to Divine justice would be unspeakably thankful for
that possession, whatever it may be, which
would cancel all his liabilities, and place
him on a level with those happy beings
who have never sinned at all. This possession is an adequate righteousness; and
if the reader be anxious to enjoy God's
favor, he will hail the gospel, for it reveals
that righteousness.

In other days, when men were in want
of money, they sometimes tried to manufacture gold. The alchymist gleaned a
portion of every possible substance from
ocean, earth, and air, and put them all into
his crucible, and then subjected the medley
to the most tedious and expensive processes.
And after days or months of watching, the
poor man was rewarded by seeing a few
grains of shining metal, and in the excitement of near discovery, the sweat stood
upon his brow, and he urged the fire afresh,
and muttered, with trembling diligence, the

spell which was to evoke the mystery.
And thus, day by day, and year by year,
with hungry face and blinking eyes, he ga-
zed into his fining-pot, and stirred the molt-
en rubbish, till one morning the neighbors
came and found the fire extinct, and the
ashes blown about, and the old alchymist
stiff, and dead, on the laboratory floor ; and
when they looked into the broken crucible,
they saw that after all his pains, the base
metals remained as base as ever.

But though men no longer endeavor to
manufacture gold, they still try to manufacture goodness. The merit which is to
open heaven, the moral excellence which
is to render God propitious, the fine gold
of righteousness, they fancy that they can
themselves elaborate. As he passed along,
the apostle Paul sometimes saw these moral
alchymists at work ; and as he observed
them so earnest for salvation—as he saw
them casting into the crucible prayers, and
alms, and tears, and fastings, and self-tor-
tures, he was moved with pity. He told

them that depraved humanity was material too base to yield the precious thing they wanted. He told them that they were spending their strength for naught; and that the merit which they were so eager to create exists already. He told them that if they would only avail themselves of it, they might obtain, without restriction, the righteousness of a Divine Redeemer. "I pray that you may be saved; I sympathize with your anxiety; I love your earnest zeal, while I deplore your deadly error. But ignorant of the righteousness which God has already provided, and going about to establish a righteousness of your own, you are missing the great magazine of merit — the great repository of righteousness — Jesus Christ. You need not scale the heavens to bring righteousness down; you need not dive into the deep in order to fetch it up; you need not watch, and toil, and do penance, in order to create it; for it exists already there. God has made his own dear Son the sinner's righteousness, and in the gospel offers him to all. The gift is nigh thee. It is at thy door; it is in thy hand. Receive it, and be righteous; receive it, and rejoice."* And so, dear reader, if you are anxious for peace with God, accept God's own gift — the peace-procuring righteousness. Present, as your only plea with a holy God, the atonement of his Son; despair of bringing merit out of vileness, or sanctity out of sin. With Luther, "learn to know Christ crucified; learn to sing a new song. Renouncing your own work, cry to Him, Lord, thou art my righteousness, and I am thy sin. Thou hast taken on thee what was mine, and given to me what was thine; what thou was not, thou becamest, that I might become what I was not."

But among the other precious commodities purchased by the Friend of Sinners, and floated to our world in that comprehensive ark, his gospel, we must notice A PEACEFUL CONSCIENCE and A CONTENTED

* Rom. x. 1–12; 1 Cor. i. 30; 2 Cor. v. 21.

4*

MIND. Should this be read by any one who has lately committed a crime, or by one who has newly discovered the holiness of God and the plague of his own heart, that reader knows the horrors of a troubled conscience. And no man can make it happy. We might put it in a palace. We might promote it to tread ankle-deep on obsequious carpets, or embosom it in balm and down. We might bid Araby breathe over it, and Golconda glitter round it. We might encircle it with clouds of hovering satellites, and put upon its head the wishing-cap of endless wealth. But if we have not taken the barb from its memory, the festered wound from the spirit—the pale foreboding, the frequent gloom, the startled slumber, will pronounce these splendors mockery, and all this luxury a glittering lie.

And even where there is not this sharp anguish, there is in the worldling's spirit a secret wretchedness, and a prevailing discontent. He longs for something, he scarce knows what; and this dim craving degenerates to a depraved voracity. He feeds on husks and ashes, or even poisonous fruits. He tries to feast his soul with fame and glory, or satiates it with sensual joys and voluptuous revelries. But from the visionary banquet he wakens up, and still his soul hath appetite; or recovered from the drunken orgy, he recognises in his besotted self a fiend imprisoned—his guilty soul the demon, and his embruted frame the dungeon. And be the diversion what it may, nothing will make a godless spirit truly happy. Get an unexpected fortune, and rise to sudden grandeur; lounge away your mornings in sumptuous club-rooms, and flutter out your evenings at balls, and plays, and operas; roam through continental vineyards or over northern moors; dawdle the long day in Brighton newsrooms, or trip it on Ramsgate pier; gallop over Ascot, or yacht it round the Needles; and from each famed resort and costly recreation, the lover of pleasure must still bring back a hollow heart and a hungry soul.

But tarry where you are — continue in your present toilsome calling; and pray that prayer, " There be many that say, Who will show us any good? Lord, lift thou up the light of thy countenance upon us, and put gladness in our heart, more than when corn and wine increase." Learn, that for Christ's sake God is reconciled to you, and life will wear another aspect. You will be like the primitive believers, after they received the remission of their sins. You will eat your meat with gladness, praising God. The same fir table is still your daily board, and from a homely trencher you still despatch your frugal meal. Work is still wearing, and winters are still severe, and still there will come hard times and heavy trials. But with heavenly entertainment at each repast, and a divine assurance deep in all your soul; in covenant with the beasts of the earth, and in league with the stones of the field, you will pass, a cheerful pilgrim, through a smiling universe, and enjoy on earth your first of heaven.

And if you ask, which package in the freight, which passage in the book, contains this priceless blessing, there are many which only need to be opened in order to obtain it. "Come now, and let us reason together, saith the Lord: Though your sins be as scarlet, they shall be as white as snow; though they be red like crimson, they shall be as wool."—"God is in Christ reconciling the world unto himself, not imputing their trespasses unto them; and hath committed unto us the word of reconciliation. Now, then, we are embassadors for Christ, as though God did beseech you by us: we pray you, in Christ's stead, be ye reconciled to God. For he hath made him to be sin for us, who knew no sin; that we might be made the righteousness of God in him."—"This is the record, that God hath given to us eternal life, and this life is in his Son. He that hath the Son hath life."

"There is no condemnation to them whc are in Christ Jesus."* Here is the am nesty, and you, my dear reader, are invited to accept it. So far as you are concerned, nothing lies nearer the heart of Jehovah than your return to his fatherly bosom ; and for this very purpose he has sent you the conditions of peace. These conditions have already been fulfilled by his own dear Son as the sinner's representative, and to that red handwriting you have only to countersign your consenting name. And no sooner do you thus fall in with God's way of saving sinners, than his beaming eye pronounces over you the benison which on earth Jesus so rejoiced to utter, "Go in peace: thy sins, which are many, be forgiven thee."

Nor must we forget that possession as precious as it is unique, THE NEW HEART. "A new heart also will I give you, and a new spirit will I put within you ; and I will take away the stony heart out of your flesh,

* Is. i. 18; 2 Cor. v. 19–21 ; 1 John v. 11, 12; Rom. viii. 1

and I will give you a heart of flesh. And
I will put my spirit within you, and will
cause you to walk in my statutes, and ye
shall keep my judgments and do them."
Whenever a man believes the gospel, God
gives him a loving, trustful, and obedient
heart; and what was formerly irksome or
odious, becomes to his altered views and
feelings attractive and easy. The Lord not
only delivers him from the slavery of sin,
and transfers him into his own family, but
gives him the cordial feelings and affectionate instincts of a son. And along with
this, everything is changed. The great
commandment, "Thou shalt love the
Lord thy God with all thy soul," is no
longer a flagrant extravagance but a gracious privilege, and the thankful spirit answers, "O Lord, thou art the strength of
my heart, and my portion for ever." Prayer
is no longer an infliction but an opportunity, and the sanctuary, from a prison or
lock-up, is transformed into a happy home-
stead and endeared resort; while the sab-

bath, once so dull or so dissipated, smiles upon him in hallowed and delightful returns. His relation to the Saviour gives a new look to the holy law ; and, receiving from the hand of a pardoning God, those requirements which he used to receive from a threatening Judge, the duties which frowned with prohibition, and coerced by penalties, become propitious and inviting. The prickly precept—" The soul that sinneth, it shall die"—the Saviour has deprived of its thorn, and along with Sharon's rose, and blending their fragrance together, he gives it to each disciple, that he may wear it in his bosom. And the harsh and hispid law — the command, which, like the loaf still latent in the bearded corn, is insipid and repulsive in the shape of dry morality—he has relieved from its choking awns and encumbering chaff ; and, sweetened with beatitude, it tastes like sacramental bread, while he himself says over it, " Eat, O friend ; yea, feast abundantly, O beloved." And as it was to his elder

Brother, it becomes to the adopted child of God like meat and drink, to do the will of his Father who is in heaven.

But, over and above its golden treasures and rich commodities, this vessel brings some RARE EXOTICS. Perfect only in that better land, there is a skilful Cultivator,* who even in these cold climes has cherished and carried through some glorious specimens. With snowy petals, and drenching all around in contagious sweetness, blooms that lily of our valley, Christian Love; and beside it, with ruby blossom, courting all the radiant firmament, holy Joy may be recognised. By its silken stem and subtle branchlets, hiding its florets from blustry weather in a pavilion of its own, Peace may be identified; while near it, Long-suffering strikes its bleeding fibres deeper, and with balm requites the hand that wounds it. As if from one source springing, Gentleness and Kindness twine together; while Faith, erect and heaven-

* Gal. v. 22; John xv. 26.

5

pointing, bears them each aloft. Scarce opening its modest eye, but bewraying its presence in the scented air, Meekness nestles in the mossy turf; and Temperance reveals in its healthy hue the tonic hidden in its root. These flowers of Paradise are sent to grace the Christian and cheer his friends; and it matters not whether they adorn the pent-up attic or the rural mansion—the spiritual mind is their true conservatory. Man's first home was a garden, and the race seems to inherit the love of those gentle shapes and glorious tints which were his silent comrades in Eden; and wandering through the sultry streets on days like these, it moves a pensive smile to see in many a window the dusty shrub or the empty flower-pot—a memento of scenes which can never be revisited, and a protest for rural joys which must not be tasted again. But those exotics which we have just enumerated, are independent of atmosphere and latitude; and some of the most splendid specimens have been cherished in workshops and cellars, amid the dust of factories, the smoke of cities, and in the depths of airless mines. "Love, joy, peace, long-suffering, gentleness, good ness, faith, meekness, temperance,"—these are the brightest beauties and the most fragrant ornaments of any dwelling. Pray that the Spirit of God would transfer them from the Bible to your character, and that he would tend and water them there. For should these graces flourish, the frost upon the fields, and the snow-flakes on the gale, will never touch the fadeless summer of your soul.

And, to notice nothing more, we must mention, as included in this costly consignment, THE TITLE-DEEDS TO A GREAT INHERITANCE. Before he left the world, the Lord Jesus said to his disciples, "In my Father's house are many mansions. I go to prepare a place for you." And the Bible gives us some hints, that we may know what sort of mansion it is. Sin and sorrow never enter it. Its inhabitant

never says, I am sick. And from his eyes
God has wiped all tears. No tempting
devil and no corrupting men come near it;
but all is holy and all is pure. Its sun
never sets, for a present Saviour is its constant light; and its blessedness never ebbs,
for God himself is the fountain of its joy.
And there the redeemed of earth have for
their company the mighty intellects and
loving souls in glory. And all this the
Saviour has purchased for his people; and
all this, happy reader, will be yours if you
belong to Jesus. Like the expiring negro,
when a friend exclaimed, " Poor Pompey!"
and he answered, " Me no poor any more,
me King Pompey now," I dare say that
you are poor, but I am sure that you are
rich. You are going where your present
rank will be no objection, and where your
earthly privations will only make the tran-
sition more ecstatic. And, oh, my friend!
look forward and look up! I wish I could
add to your present comforts; but I know
that if you had it, this blessed hope would

often cheat your present miseries. One windy afternoon I went with a friend into a country almshouse. There was sitting before a feeble fire a very aged man; and the better to keep from his bald head the cold gusts, he wore his hat: he was never likely to need it out of doors. He was very deaf, and so shaken with the palsy, that one wooden shoe constantly pattered on the brick floor. But, deaf, and sick, and helpless, it turned out that he was happy. "What are you doing, Wisby?" said my friend. "Waiting, sir." "And for what?" "For the appearing of my Lord." "And what makes you wish for his appearing?" "Because, sir, I expect great things then. He has promised a crown of righteousness to all that love his appearing." And, to see whether it was a right foundation on which he rested that glorious hope, we asked old Wisby what it was. By degrees he got on his spectacles, and opening the great Bible beside him, pointed to that text, "Therefore, being justified by faith, we

5*

have peace with God through our Lord
Jesus Christ: by whom also we have access by faith into this grace wherein we
stand, and rejoice in hope of the glory of
God."* And, dear reader, the God of
grace puts that blessedness within your
offer. Embrace it, and you will be the
happy man "to whom death is welcome,
while life is sweet."

> " When I can read my title clear
>   To mansions in the skies,
>   I bid farewell to every fear,
>   And wipe my weeping eyes."

And now, kind reader, have you understood these things? Over a few sentences
of this address, I have cast a thin veil of
metaphor;—but I shall be very sorry if it
has obscured my meaning; for even in
these humble pages, there are truths which,
if you believe and embrace, you need envy
no man's millions, and many a wealthy
worldling is poor compared with you.

The thing which I have been most
anxious to show, is the kind tone in which

* Rom. v. 1, 2.

the Saviour speaks to you, and the boons
which, in the Bible, he transmits to you.
Judging by some sermons and tracts, you
might fancy that the Bible is a severe and
angry book—or, at the very best, that it is a
book of good advices. This is a mistake.
The Bible has many a solemn passage, and
it abounds in good advices; but you miss
the very best of it if you think that this is
all. I shall suppose that a young man has
left his home in Scotland or the north of
England. He comes to this great London,
and in a little while falls in with its worst
ways. In the theatre, and the tea-garden,
and the tavern parlor, he spends all his
money, and gets deep in debt; and then
he turns ill, and is taken to the hospital;
and when there, he begins to bethink him
of his foolishness: "I wish I once were
well again. I wish I once were home
again. But 'tis no use wishing. I know
that my father's door is shut: they would
not take me in; and if once I were
able to creep about, they would have me

up for debt. It would just oe out of the
hospital into the jail." And, while be-
moaning his misery, a letter comes from his
father, telling him that he has heard of his
wretched plight, and reminding him of the
past, and all he had done for his wayward
child ; and, glancing his eye over it, the sick
youth crumples it up and crams it away under his pillow. And by-and-by a comrade
comes in, and among other things the invalid
tells him, " And here is a letter of good
advice just come from my father ;" and that
other runs his eye over it: " Good advice,
did you say? I think you should rather
have said good news. Don't you see, he
makes you welcome home again? and in
order that you may settle your accounts,
and return in peace and comfort, he has
appended this draft for twenty pounds."
Most people read the Bible carelessly, or
with a guilty conscience for the interpreter,
and they notice in it nothing but reproofs
and good advice. They miss the main
thing there. The gospel is good news.

It tells us that God is love, and announces to every reader that the door of the Father's house is open, and that this very night he may fiud a blessed home in the bosom of his God. And as we have all incurred a debt to Divine justice, which, throughout eternity, we could never pay—and as it needs a righteousness to recommend us to the favor of a holy God—in every Bible there is enclosed a draft on the Saviour's merit, to which the sinner has only to sign his believing name, and the great salvation is his own. By exhibiting the cross of Christ—by directing to that precious blood which cleanses from all sin—and by presenting a perfect righteousness to every awakened conscience—the Bible comes a benefactor and a friend in need. And when rightly understood, the angelic anthem—" Glory to God in the highest; on earth peace ; good-will toward man"—is the cheerful but stately tune to which the gospel goes, and to which in heaven itself they sing it.

And, reader, try to catch that tune. Pray
that God would this very night, by his own
Spirit, teach it to you. Fear not to believe
too soon, nor to rejoice in Christ Jesus too
much. Let the love of God your Saviour
tide into all your soul, and, as it makes
your feelings happy, so will it make your
dispositions new. Peace and joy will keep
you from some sins, gratitude and loyalty
will preserve you from the rest. No cheerful glass will be needed to raise your spirits then ; for a soul exulting in the great
salvation forgets its poverty, and remembers its misery no more. No sinful lust
nor forbidden joy will enthral you then ; for
you will have discovered deeper and purer
pleasures. And there will be no fear of
your growling and cursing through your
daily task, or filling with consternation your
cowering family ; for the peace of God will
make **you** pacific, and scattering on every
side kind looks and friendly feelings, you
will come and go a sunshine in the shop, a
firelight in the home.

No: do not sit so sullenly. I am a
stranger, but it is the truth of God I tell.
In all your life you may never have got a
costly gift; but here, at last, is one. It is
the gift of God, and therefore it is a gift
unspeakable; but, accepted as cordially as
it is graciously offered, it will make you
blessed now, and rich for all eternity. Oh,
my dear friend, do not eye it so coldly;
suffer it not so tamely to pass away. This
night has brought you good news. It has
told you of the Saviour's costly purchase
and wondrous present. Let it also bring
good news to heaven; let it tell that the
love of God has broken your heart, and
made you sorry and ashamed for all your
sins; let it tell that with tears of thankfulness you have surveyed the " unsearchable
riches of Christ," and have given yourself
to Him who once gave himself for you; let
it tell that your history has taken a new
turn, and that, breaking off from your worthless companions and evil ways, you have
begun in lowliness and love to follow Jesus

A BUNCH IN THE HAND, AND MORE ON THE BUSH.

Not far from this London there dwelt an old couple. In early life they had been poor; but the husband became a Christian, and God blessed their industry, and they were living in a comfortable retirement, when one day a stranger called on them to ask their subscription to a charity. The old lady had not so much grace as her husband, and still hankered after some of the sabbath earnings and easy shillings which Thomas had forfeited from regard to the law of God. And so when the visiter asked their contribution, she interposed, and said, "Why, sir, we have lost a deal by religion since we first began; my husband knows that very well. Have we not, Thomas?" And after a solemn pause Thomas an-

swered : " Yes, Mary, we have. I have lost
a deal by my religion. Before I had got religion, Mary, I had got a water-pail, in which
I used to carry water, and that, you know, I
have lost many years ago ; and then I had
an old slouched hat, a tattered coat, and
mended shoes and stockings ; but I have
lost them also long ago. And, Mary, you
know that, poor as I was, I had a habit of
getting drunk and quarreling with you ; and
that, you know, I have lost. And then I
had a burdened conscience and a wicked
heart, and ten thousand guilty fears ; but
all are lost, completely lost, and like a mill-
stone, cast into the deepest sea. And,
Mary, you have been a loser too, though
not so great a loser as myself. Before we
got religion, Mary, you had got a washing-
tray, in which you washed for hire ; but
since we got religion, you have lost your
washing-tray. And you had a gown and a
bonnet much the worse for wear, though
they were all you had to wear ; but you
have lost them long ago. And you had

6

many an aching heart concerning me at
times; but these you happily have lost.
And I could even wish that you had lost
as much as I have lost; for what we lose
by our religion will be our everlasting gain."

There are instances where religion has
required a sacrifice; but so far as our own
observation goes, it has blessed its posses-
sors, not only by what it imparted, but also
by what it took away.   Their chief losses
may be comprised in the following items :—

A bad character;

A guilty conscience;

A troublesome temper;

Sundry evil habits,

And all their wicked companions.

And then, on the other side, over and
above all the higher benefits which the gospel bestows, and which, in our last paper,
we tried to enumerate, its advent into the
poor man's home is usually signalized by
some immediate and obvious blessings. We
allow that they are secondary, but they are
not insignificant.   Let us glance at some

of them. Like the bunch which the spies
fetched from Eshcol, they may give some
notion of the goodly land; but they are
only a sample, and the true wisdom is to
go up and possess the region itself, and then
you will gather the grapes where they grow,
and when one cluster is finished, you will
find still better on the tree.

1. Religion is FORETHOUGHT and FRU-
GALITY. The disciple of Jesus is well
off—his fortune is made, and he does not
need to set his heart on filthy lucre. But
then he is high-hearted—he is of his Master's mind, " It is more blessed to give than
to receive." He would rather be an almo-
ner than a pensioner; and he is anxious
to lay a good foundation for age as well as
for infirmity. And he " provides for his
own house." He would fain contribute to
the commonwealth one independent and
self-sustaining family. And the foresight
and self-denial which he has learned at the
feet of Jesus, put these achievements in
his power. You may see the thing in liv-

ing specimens. Take, for instance, these shopmates, Dick Raspiron and Tom Tinkleton. Perhaps you know them; at all events, in their employment as whitesmiths they have made some noise in the world. Tom once of a sudden took it into his head to marry; and as he had a few shillings to pay the fees, he made it out; but before the honeymoon was ended, the bride had to pawn her wedding-gown to buy next Sunday's dinner. And Dick also fell in love; but his sweetheart and himself agreed that they would wait till they had made up twenty pounds between them. Last Saturday Tom did not take home his wages till after midnight, and then he did not take the whole; and next morning his wife went out and bought some flabby meat and withered greens, and paid the Sunday trader ten per cent. additional; but that was better management than the time before, for then he brought nothing home at all; and in order to procure a steak, they had first to sell their frying-pan. But now that at

last he has married his notable little wife,
Dick hies home as fast as he can on Saturday evening, sure that the earnings of last
week have made the marketings of this one,
and that he will find the room so tidy and
the tea-things set out, and that afterward
they will have a turn in the park, or, should
it chance to rain, an hour for reading some
useful book.   At an immemorial period his
shopmate "fell behind;" that is, in a certain race, the consumer of pies and porter
outran the producer of water-pails and me-
tallic chimney-pots; and the shillings which
he got from his employer could not keep
up with the half-crowns which he spent on
himself.   And ever since the luckless day
when the Spender distanced the Winner,
it has been a perpetual scramble.   For want
of ready cash—and credit they never
had—his hungry household subsists on accidental and precarious meals; and bought
in paltry shops, and in the smallest quan-
tities, their greatest bargain is a stinted pen-
nyworth.   Richard read in his Bible, "Owe

no man anything;" and, in order to make sure, he thought it best to have always something to spare. At the very outset he bade the Winner " march," while he held the Spender by the heel, and would not let him stir a single step till the other was far ahead. And now he begins to find the advantage of this early self-denial. From having a little money at command, he has never on an emergency required to borrow at a ruinous usury, and he has been able to pick up at a trifling cost a clock and a bookcase, and a chest of drawers, when they happened to be going cheap. And he has discovered that sovereigns are, in their habits, somewhat gregarious; if, like rats, they run away from a tottering house, like storks and starlings they are ready to come and colonize wherever one of their species reports a kind reception. And accordingly, with little exertion, without pinching or scraping, or any shabby expedients, he finds the little store quietly increasing. And now it is whispered in the street, that he either means to lease or buy the house in which he has been heretofore a lodger; while during the year his neighbor has effected three removals. And curious observers have noted that each of these removals is less ex-pensive than its predecessor; and it is likely that the next may cost nothing, as at the present rate they will then be able to carry on their backs all their remaining goods and chattels.

In providing for one's own house, perhaps the best plan is mutual insurance. In many provident societies the premiums have been calculated too low; but in some recently established, such as the " Christian Mutual Provident Society," a scale of payments has been adopted, which effectually secures against all risk. I shall suppose that the reader is a healthy man, and twenty-five years of age. Would he like to secure ten shillings a week, during every term of sickness, for the next forty years? He may secure it by paying 1s. $4\frac{1}{2}d$. a month, or a halfpenny every day. Or would he like to retire from hard work at the end of these forty years? By paying 2s. 3d. monthly, or less than a penny daily, he may buy against that period a pension of 6s. weekly. Or would he prefer leaving to his survivors, at whatever time it may please God to call him away, a sum of solid money? For such a purpose he may secure 100l. by paying 3s. 5d. a month, or 2l. a year. Or, if he dislikes insurance, he may try the savings' bank, and there the daily penny would mount up to 50l. in thirty years.

But how is a working man to manage this? How is he to spare the daily penny from his scanty earnings? I fear some can not; but I know that many can. Do you smoke, or snuff, or chew tobacco? Then please to count how much this costs you in a week, and how much in the fifty-two weeks which make a year. And how much do you pay for stimulating liquor? A friend reminds me that a moderate pint of beer comes to 3l. per annum, or 30l. in ten years. And how do you dispose of your loose half-pence? And how much do you spend in Sunday excursions, and fairs, and treats, and merry-makings? Not very much on any one occasion, but enough from time to time to make at last a fortune. For it is not by surprising windfalls, but by systematic savings—by the resolute repetition of Jane Taylor's golden maxim, "I can do without it,"—that men have made the most solid fortunes, the fullest of satisfaction to the founder, and the most enduring. And were you only commencing now to save up the coppers which you have hitherto squandered at the pastrycook's or the fruiterer's stall, and the sixpences which you would have melted in beer or burned in tobacco, they will soon swell up to a pound; and by perseverance and the blessing of God, that pound may grow to a competency.*

* We would cordially recommend to our readers on this and kindred subjects, Chambers' Penny Tract, No. 170, "Hints to Workmen." After the above paragraphs were written, a friend in the west of England was kind enough to show us over his factory. It abounded in contrivances and processes which we had never seen before; but the sight which interested us beyond all

2. Religion insures SOBRIETY. Is it
not fearful that Britain spends on intoxi-
cating liquors fifty millions every year?
We often complain of our high taxation,
and sometimes grow nervous at the national
debt. But here is a tax for which we can-
not blame our rulers; a tax self-imposed
and self-levied; a tax for which we can only
blame ourselves; a tax which would pay the
interest of our national debt twice over;
and a tax as large as the entire revenue of
these United Kingdoms. We thought it a
great sum to pay in order to give the slave
his freedom; we thought the twenty millions given to the West India proprietors

these was a picture-gallery of industrious veterans. In
his counting-room the warm-hearted proprietor had sus-
pended, large as life, the portraits of five faithful servants, who had each spent about half a century in these
works. I need not say that they had been all sober
men. It was a rule of the establishment, that no one
employed at it should ever enter a public-house. But
most of these venerable worthies had been pious men;
and, pointing to one of the likenesses, my friend mentioned, "That old man was worth fifteen hundred
pounds when he died." He was a common worker with
ordinary wages; but he realized enough to provide a com
fortable independence for two nieces who survive him.

a mighty sacrifice; and certainly it was the noblest tribute any nation ever paid to the cause of philanthropy: but, large as it looks, half a year of national abstinence would have paid it all. Some grudge the eight millions which Ireland lately got, seeing it failed to set our neighbors on their feet;—but it was eight millions given to save a famishing people; and large as the grant to Ireland sounds, two months of national abstinence would have paid the whole of it. But, tremendous as are the fifty millions which, as a people, we yearly ingulf in strong drink, the thought which afflicts and appals us is that this terrible impost is mainly a tax on the working man. The lamentation is that many an industrious man will spend in liquor as much money as, had he saved it, would this year have furnished a room, and next year would have bought a beautiful library;—as much money as would secure a splendid education for every child, or in the course of a few years would have made him a landlord instead of a tenant. Why, my friends, it would set our blood a-boiling if we heard that the Turkish sultan taxed his subjects in the style that our British workmen tax themselves. It would bring the days of Wat Tyler back again—nay, it would create another Hampden, and conjure up a second Cromwell—did the exchequer try to raise the impost which our publicans levy, and our laborers and artisans cheerfully pay. But is it not a fearful infatuation? Is it not our national madness to spend so much wealth in shattering our nerves, and exploding our characters, and ruining our souls? Many workmen, I rejoice to know, have been reclaimed by teetotalism, and many have been preserved by timely religion. In whatever way a man is saved from that horrible vice, which is at once the destruction of the body and the damnation of the soul, " therein I do rejoice, and will rejoice." Only you can not be a Christian without being also a sober man; and the more of God's grace you get, the easier will you find it to vanquish this most terrible of the working man's temptations.

3. Religion creates HONESTY, CIVILITY, PUNCTUALITY, INDUSTRY, and those other qualities which secure for the working man popularity and promotion. And, whatever theorists may propound to the contrary, this is the way in which God himself has arranged society. The steady and sober are to rise and be respected, while the dissolute and disorderly must sink and disappear. And though there is in many quarters a prejudice against piety — though some infidel and irreligious employers prefer workmen with easy principles and pliant consciences — no business can long prosper without probity, and no employer can become permanently rich with ruffians or rogues for his servants. Hence, in all extensive and protracted undertakings, principle will undoubtedly win for itself an eventual preference; aud the workman who understands his trade and keeps his character, may expect to retain his place. The

7

king of Babylon had no liking for Daniel's religion; but then, Daniel was the only man who could manage the hundred provinces. And the king of Egypt would have preferred Joseph's finance and Joseph's forethought without Joseph's piety; but, as he could not get the one without the other, he put up with the Hebrew's faith for the sake of the statesman's policy. And in the same way, if you carry Bible rules into your conduct, the Lord himself will undertake your case, and people will find out that it is good to have the like of you around them. If you will not work on Sunday, neither will you be tipsy or a-missing on Monday. If you won't tell a falsehood for your employer, neither will you waste his materials nor pilfer his property. And if you are not a sycophant in the slackest times, you will not be saucy in the busiest; but, seeking first to please your Master in heaven, you will find yourself rewarded with the good will and confidence of your superiors on earth.

Richard Williams attended the Horshay iron works, in Shropshire. From the time that he found the forgiveness of his sins at the foot of the cross, he became a delightful neighbor and a most diligent workman. He was a methodist, and his master a quaker; and seeing Richard's conscientiousness, Mr. Reynolds promoted him to be one of his superintendents — an office which he held with growing honor all his life. One secret of Richard's promotion, and one reason why whatsoever he did prospered well, was his prayerfulness. God was his heavenly Father, and therefore he besought his blessing on his common toils; and I think you will be interested to read the two following letters to a friend :—

"I am much better in health to-day, but am in some difficulty as to our works. We are 'setting on' the other furnace, and it goes off very stubbornly. It requires a deal of care and hard work to get it right; and will require much more, unless a speedy turn takes place in our favor. Continue, therefore, to pray for us. I know your prayers will do more than all we can do with our strong bars and great hammers. Do not, therefore, forget us at the throne of the heavenly grace."

Again :—

" We are engaged in difficult work, and are desirous of getting it over before sabbath. I pray the Lord that we may succeed. The expenses of the works to Mr Reynolds are at present very great, and the profits none. I am employed all night and a part of the day; but I heartily thank God for his kind care over me, and hope he will preserve us all. Very earnestly do I wish that we may get it done, that we all may have the sabbath free from labor for the purposes of religion."

And his love of the sabbath and his personal consistency were at last rewarded, by seeing every furnace stopped on the first day of the week. On a subject so near his heart, he ventured a respectful representation to the proprietor—a representation

which derived such weight from Richard's
worth and modesty, that, notwithstanding
the pecuniary hazard, an experiment was
permitted: it proved successful; and these
sabbatic furnaces are a noble monument to
a conscientious working man.

The truth is, that God's blessing attends
his people in their common calling. If
they commit their way to him, he brings
it to pass. He opens doors. He finds
for them friends and favor. He smooths
down difficulties, and gives their earnings
reproductive value. You have likely heard
of Thomas Mann, the London waterman.
Besides large sums given in his life to poor
acquaintances, he left to different societies
nearly two thousand pounds. And how
did he make it? God gave it to him.
God gave him great faith in his own word
and promises — a devout and God-fearing
mind; and these developed in politeness
and honesty, punctuality and diligence.
People who once used his boat were so
taken with its owner, that if they could get

him again, they would hail no other; and
having won a friend, he was so attentive
and exact that he never lost him again;
and though he never plied on the Sabbath,
and never pocketed a shilling beyond the
proper fare, and was always giving money
away, it seemed as if he could not grow
poor.   Always sober, always cheerful, and
usually the first on the water, the Lord
smiled on his pious industry; and, amid all
his prosperity, the Lord kept him humble
and generous, to show us that if a man has
already got heaven in his heart, a handful
of money will not make him a miser.

4. Religion is REFINEMENT. It expands
the mind of its possessor, and purifies his
taste.   It is a great mistake to confound
riches and refinement, just as it is a great
mistake to fancy that because a man is poor,
he must be coarse and vulgar.   Lord Jef-
feries, though seated on the highest tribunal
in the realm, while pouring forth his brutal
ribaldry, was a vulgar man; and a very
vulgar man was Chancellor Thurlow, sport-

ing oaths and obscenity at the table of the prince of Wales. But there was no vulgarity about James Ferguson, though herding sheep, while his eye watched Arcturus and the Pleiades, and his wistful spirit wandered through immensity; and, though seated at a stocking-loom, there was no vulgarity in the youth who penned the " Star of Bethlehem;" the weaver-boy, Henry Kirke White, was not a vulgar lad. Aud so, my respected friends, if you surrender your minds to the teaching of God's word and Spirit, they will receive the truest, deepest refinement. There may be nothing in your movements to indicate the training of the dancing-school, nor anything in your elocution which speaks of courtly circles or smooth society; but there will be an elevation in your tastes, and a purity in your feelings, as of men accustomed to the society of the King of kings You will have a relish for a higher litera ture than the halfpenny ballad or the Sunday news, and for a more improving intercourse than the tap or the club room can supply. And though you may not have at easy command the phrases of politeness, the most polished, if they but be the children of God, will have sentiments and language in common with you, and a stronger affinity for you than for the most fine-spoken impiety. And in your respectful demeanor to those above you, and in your kind and civil carriage to those around you, men will see that you have learned your manners from the book which says, " Be courteous," and which supplies the finest model of gentility. The religion which is at last to lift the beggar from the dunghill, and set him with nobles of the earth, will even now give the toiling man the elevated aims, the enlarged capacity, the lofty tastes, and manly bearing, which princes have often lacked ; for if vice be the worst vulgarity, religion is the best refinement.

5. Religion secures that priceless possession — a HAPPY HOME. Six things are requisite to create a home. Integrity must

be the architect, and Tidiness the upholsterer. It must be warmed by Affection, and lighted up with Cheerfulness; and Industry must be the ventilator, renewing the atmosphere, and bringing in fresh salubrity day by day; while over all, as a protecting canopy and defending glory, nothing will suffice except the blessing of God.

Dear reader, if you are in earnest yourself, I hope it is your privilege to have a pious partner. If not, "what knowest thou, O man, but that by prayer and persuasion thou mayest gain thy wife?" And then all will work sweetly; and with the Bible to direct you, and helping one another, you may condense into your dwelling, however narrow, all the happiness of which this mortal state is susceptible.

In the north of England, and in the days of haunted houses, a certain farm was infested by a mischievous sprite. It skimmed the milk, and soured the cream; it made the haystacks heat, and blasted the cattle into skin and bone; and besides frightening the maid-servants, and tumbling the children into the pond, it often raised such a riot up among the rafters, that the poor people were brought to their wits' end, and resolved on leaving the place. Everything was packed, and the cavalcade was in motion; and they had proceeded so far in their journey when a countryman met the procession, and in amazement demanded, "What's thee doing, neighbor Hodge?" "We are flitting," shouted the farmer, gruffly; and from the depths of the wagon a shrill voice echoed, "Yes, WE are flitting;" and at the same moment one of the youngsters screamed, "Oh, father, father, Brownie's in the churn!" And finding that their foe was as ready for the road as themselves, the farmer turned the horse's head, and went back to his old premises with a look of woful resignation. And in the course of my travels I have often encountered a Brownie's flitting. Beneath the shadow of the Drachenfels, on Loch-lomond's silvery tide, in the fluttering

streets of Paris, and on the bright mountains of Wales, I have many times fallen in
with a family party, evidently fleeing from
a haunted house. And having devoted
some attention to the subject, I find that
the mansions of the aristocracy are mainly
frequented by two evil spirits, called Indifference and Ennui. They are dull de-
mons, both of them, quite different from
the vivacious Brownies of the farm and the
village : they raise no racket overhead ; but
being of phlegmatic mood and courtly habits,
they wear felt slippers and glide softly over
the polished floor. The one is an incubus
which dulls the heart, the other a torpedo
which benumbs the brain. Indifference or
Nonchalance (for both he and his cousin
Ennui are foreigners, and had French
names when they first came over)—Indifference takes the zest from friendship, and
all the endearment out of closest kindred.
If he gets into the breakfast-parlor, my lady
and my lord have nothing to say to one another, but my lord takes alternate mouth-

fuls of his muffin and the morning paper,
and my lady communes in silence with the
sugar-tongs; and if he gets into the nursery,
the brothers and sisters there are blighted
into little lords and little ladies, with as
little love to one another as if they were
already old; and if they love papa and
mamma, it is because they have learned
to connect them with the cake and fruit
which endear the moments after dinner.
And Ennui is an idle ghost, harboring under ottomans and sofas, fond of a dressing-
gown, and delighting in breakfasts at mid-
day; and a most irksome ghost—a sort of
aerial cuttle, shedding inky gloom into the
atmosphere, and blackening the brightest
skies—a moral Remora,* frustrating existence, and leaving clever and accomplished
people without an object and without an

*The press-corrector has put a query at this word;
and perhaps the reader will put another. It was a fish
which, in the time of Pliny, could stop a ship in full
sail. But, as it is no longer known to seamen, I sus-
pect, as hinted above, that it has exchanged the stormy
deep for our modern drawing-rooms.

effort, becalmed on a carpet, spell-bound on a woollen sea.

> " Day after day, day after day,
>   They stick, nor breath nor motion ;
>   As idle as a painted ship
>   Upon a painted ocean."

And it is to escape from these afflictive inmates that the travelling-carriage is ordered to the door, and the rumble put on. But all in vain. The Brownies have bespoken their seats. The one perks his long visage between my lord and lady, and the other mounts the box with the heir apparent. The country is deplorably " stupid ;" and as the day wears on, the travellers discover many omissions and " tiresome" mistakes, which are so far a relief as entitling them to be cross at one another ; and when the sumptuous hotel is attained, and the costly dinner despatched, a sullen sprite guides each to his chamber and laughs as they labor to sleep—

> " For vainly Betty performs her part,
>   If a ruffled head and a rumpled heart,
>   As well as the couch, want making."

8

And I am sorry to add that many a cottage is haunted. The circumstance which first called my attention to the fact, was finding that so few working-people are keepers at home. In the evenings, I found them at penny-theatres, and at "judge and jury" trials, smoking beside the alehouse fire, or lounging over a tankard at the door of some country-tavern. And I was sorry to see them. I regretted that they should be so selfish. I grieved that they should indulge in enjoyments in which their wives and children could not share. But going to their houses, I found a reason. I found that many of these husbands and fathers were driven from their homes by evil spirits. The truth is, that the abode of many an industrious man is rendered miserable by two notorious goblins, and they are none the better for being native Saxons. Tawdriness is a sluttish fairy, rejoicing in dirt and disorder; her sandals are down in the heels, the better to display the gap in the stocking-sole; and a tuft of ragged hair

asserts its freedom through a corresponding
rent in the frowzy cap. In matters of
vertu—in pottery and furniture—her taste
is for torsos and fractured specimens, chairs
without bottoms, and grates without bars,
and therefore she breaks the spouts of the
pitchers, and burns the nozzle of the bellows and the brush of the hearthbroom.
And in the picturesque, her liking is for
new combinations and striking contrasts; a
blazing riband and a smutty face; a feed
to-day and a fast to-morrow. On one end
of her geographical tea-table, untouched
since the morning, England is represented
in crumbs of bread, and alongside, the sister isle is symbolized in potato-parings; and
at another corner, an Arve of muddy ale
mingles with a Rhone of reluctant sky-
blue. The kindred elf is Turmoil. Her
talent lies in creating discord; and between
the slamming of the door, and the clashing
of the fire-irons, and the squalling of tur-
bulent children, it is not surprising that she
sometimes scares away to other scenes the

distracted " good man of the house." The
two together are more than a match for any
man ; and we can not wonder at the strange
asylums which people seek whose homes
are haunted by dirtiness and din.

But all these foes of the house disappear
when piety takes possession. I could rejoice to tell the scenes which may be wit-
nessed in some of England's stately halls,
where the genius of the place is an ascend-
ant gospel, and where, from its presence,
listlessness and languor have fled away.
Because I think you would like to look at
them, I would gladly sketch some of these
bright moral spectacles, where, surrounded
by the beauties of nature and t:ie amenities
of art, families of high degree dwell lovingly together, and occupy their hours in
intellectual improvement and in devices for
doing good to those around them ; where
wealth gives practical expression to philanthropy, and where the morning and evening sacrifice derive, not virtue, but impres-
siveness from their position who present it

But I must indulge in no more digression. I must hasten to tell how real religion would make your homes happy, my dear, industrious neighbors.

And, for one thing, it would make them neat and tidy. The mind of an ungodly man is all confusion. Whims and fancies, lusts and passions, come and go; and there being no pervasive principle, no holy controlling power, no master of the house, that mind becomes a perfect chaos — a cage of disorder and impurity. And that mind manifests itself. It is very apt to transfer its own image to the abode in which it dwells, and make this also a den of filth and confusion. But as soon as that mind surrenders to the spirit of God, and is possessed by this heavenly inmate, a mighty change comes over it. He shuts the door against vile thoughts and vilianous notions; and refractory passions he quells beneath his firm but gentle sway. And he creates a liking for what is pure, honest, lovely, and of good report. And that inward change

8*

tells outwardly — the renewed mind shows itself. It sets the house in order; it finds a place for everything, and keeps everything in its place; and though it may not afford costly raiment or fine furniture, it is rich enough to keep them clean.

And just as it purifies the house, so religion pacifies the household. A great calm inwardly, it sheds a tranquillizing influence on every side. It fills the hearts which hold it with love to one another, and to happy yokefellows it gives a truer and more tender understanding than ever sprang from sentimental fondness.

The man of prayer is always a man of power. His very presence is encircled by a serene ascendency, and his children and all around him feel it. His own happiness reminds him that there is a time to laugh and a time to play; and instead of fretting at childish glee, he can heartily promote it. Or if it be time to forbear, his friendly "Hush!" creates an instant and cheerful calm. The man of prayer carries with him

something of that secret majesty which is
only gotten at the mercy-seat; and while
he is not seeking to bend all things to his
imperious wishes, he finds his wishes fore-
stalled, and his desires fulfilled by prompt
affection, or, better still, by a kind and all-
controlling power. And, hastening from
his daily toil, he knows what he may expect within — smiles and caresses, and
schoolroom news, loud shouts and silent
love — shouts which tell that the father is
not formidable, and silent love, which can
not tell how dear the husband is, but both
together telling to his inmost heart the lov
ing-kindness of the Lord.

Reader, your happiness will be my
reward. In this paper I have tried to
show, that, even within the limits of the
present life, there is great gain in contented godliness. Will you not try it?
Will you not be persuaded to that wise
experiment which thousands have made,
but never one regretted?

Think over what I have written. Read it to your wife. Ask her what she thinks, and should you both agree that your present course is not the best, and that it might be mended, begin at once the more excellent way.

Pray to God that, for Jesus's sake, he would give you the teaching of his own Holy Spirit. You have many things to learn; many bad habits to give up, and many good ones to begin. You can do nothing of yourselves; but may the Lord make you able and willing in his day of power!

For the past, seek pardon in a Saviour's blood. If urged in the Mediator's name, God will not despise the prayer. " Wash me from mine iniquity, and cleanse me from my sin. Create in me a clean heart, O God; and renew a right spirit within me."

And, for the future, resolve, in the strength of the Lord, on a course of conduct entirely new. Say with the Psalmist, " I will behave myself wisely in a perfect

way; I will walk within my house with a
perfect heart. A froward heart shall de-
part from me; I will not know a wicked
person.

And, to show that you are sincere—to
prevent your present purposes from melting
like the vanished goodness of other days,—
take action. This evening set up God's
worship in your family.* Next Lord's
day carry your household to some Christian sanctuary, and commence a course of
constant attendance on the means of grace.
Break instantly with any bad companions,
and if there be anything on which you
covet farther light, consult some missionary, or minister, or pious friend. And
may the Lord bless you, and keep you,
and cause his countenance to shine upon
you !

* Those who wish directions for conducting this
blessed service, which has given a new and joyful aspect
to many a dwelling, are referred to a tract, called " The
Church in the House."

[This tract is published with some others in the
" Harp on the Willow."—Am. Pub.]

"O God of Bethel! by whose hand
　　Thy people still are fed,
Who through this weary pilgrimage
　　Hast all our fathers led:

"Through each perplexing path of life
　　Our wand'ring footsteps guide;
Give us each day our daily bread,
　　And raiment fit provide.

"O spread thy cov'ring wings around,
　　Till all our wand'rings cease,
And at our Father's loved abode,
　　Our souls arrive in peace."

THE BATTLE OF WATERLOO.

THE GUN OR THE GOSPEL.

NOT long ago we went to look at Waterloo — and Waterloo looked at us. Like
most of the storied places which we have
chanced to visit, he seemed to remember
all about himself, and told us a deeper tale
than the old sergeant who acted as our
guide and his interpreter. We found him
nearly recovered from the rough usage of
the famous conflict. His right arm, the
scorched and battered Hougomont, he still
carries in a sling; and a huge excrescence
has grown up where the shots fell thickest:
while solemn monuments are the scars
which cover many a casualty On the
whole, however, the veteran wore a placid
aspect. His crops were in good condition,
and he had lately taken to the bleaching
trade; and though one of our party was
hunting a rare butterfly on the very mount

of the Belgic lion, he did not resent the levity. Even Waterloo, though pensively, appeared to share the spirit of the age, and gave his vote for traffic, peace, and progress.

And since that day, in quiet hours, the old Battlefield will often come to us and talk to us. And, reader, we shall confide to thee some lessons which the gray warrior has whispered in our inward ear.

Sometimes he says, " Be thankful. It was no common fight: it was not a play of arms; it was not the old tournay betwixt France and England, with a little glory for the prize. But it was an Armageddon. It was a battle betwixt freedom and brute force — betwixt the soul of man and military despotism, — and a battle of most anxious issue. In men and guns, the oppressor was much the strongest. His troops spoke one language, were moved by one intelligence, and, familiar with victory, they were this time flushed with vindictive fury. The allies came from all countries. As he

marched beneath the beech-trees of Soig-
nies, or rose from his rainy bivouac that
morning, many a soldier felt for the first
time that he was about to stand, front to
front, with death; and even the bravest
were taken aback by the enemy's rapid
arrival. And had some little move been
different—had not heavier metal been introduced into the British artillery—had
the Belgian panic spread—had the frail
defence of Hougomont yielded—had Na-
poleon not wavered at a critical conjunc-
ture—had the English guards failed to
repel the charge of his veterans—or had
the Prussians been a little later in coming,—
the story of the world might have bounded
back a hundred years, and, like another
Sisyphus, weary Europe would have been
constrained to moil up hill once more the
stone which bluff Harry and grand Louis
had twice before rolled down. But the
Lord on high controlled it all. He gave
the timely valor; he brought the season-
able succor; he prompted the previous

9

plans, and crowned them with prosperity;
he toned the nerves on which freedom
hung; and when a few miles and a single
day were all that intervened betwixt Europe and an age of steel, he smote the
spoiler, and gave the nations what they
never knew before — a generation of peace
and improvement; an era of busy enterprise and bloodless industry, an age of
intelligence, and liberty, and lofty aspira-
tions."

Sometimes, in accents more subdued,
our oracle will say, " Be thankful, for war
is fearful work. You are a youngster, and
have forgotten it, and it is easy for you to
sit under your fig-tree, and read it in Ali-
son or Siborne; but you can never realize
it. That morning, the people at home rose
from pleasant slumber, and little knew what
thousands, over-night, could boast no better
bed than the flooded fields of Mont St.
Jean. And when the village bells were
sprinkling sabbath music over all the land,
and the psalm of praise pealed high, they

did not hear the death-shots rattle and the murdering cannons roar. And when the Sunday-schools were met, and family groups repeated hymns and read the word of God together, they were not startled by the noise as bombs exploded, and frantic squadrons swooped at one another in trampling thunder. And when Highland cottagers knelt down for evening worship, and London streets were brightly filled from closing sanctuaries, none knew that their fathers and brothers strewed the turf where the tide of battle had receded, and left behind its wreck of surging agony. Distance of place made people unconscious, and therefore callous, then; distance of time makes you almost as unconscious and as callous now. But, trust me, war is ghastly work, and I never shall forget that night of horrors. I can not forget the shudder of mother Earth as her dying children tossed upon her bosom, and how timidly from among the clouds the moon peeped forth on miles of slain. I can not forget the

moans, and blasphemies, and prayers. I
can not forget how the stalwart grenadier
would spurn the sod, and grasp the clay in
his terrible death-struggle; and how softly
the warm blood flowed through the broid-
ered vest of the gallant youth, till England
and his sisters stood before his eyes, and
melted into his swooning sleep.* And,
sooth to say, broad-cast with orphanage
and widowhood as that evening left my
acres, it was long before I felt the pride
of glorious victory." But lately our mystic
visiter came to us in more cheerful mood.
It was a sabbath morning, and the 18th of
June in the bygone summer; and along
with the dim light the wraith of Waterloo
stole into our chamber. "I wish you joy,"
said the vision; "a new thing in the earth!
Europe completes this day a generation of

* Those who would like to know how it fares with
the wounded soldier on the field of battle, may read the
narrative of Colonel Ponsonby as given in Gleig's story
of Waterloo. It is too long for transcription here; but
Mr. Gilbert has told most of it in the sketch which
precedes this paper.

repose! Britain has kept peace for three and thirty years! To you and your coevals the lines have fallen in pleasant places; and for your lot in this wealthiest and happiest of all times, you can not thank enough the Prince of Peace. Diluted and indirect, there is a gospel in this age; and if you can get the ear of any of your countrymen, go and tell them the blessings of this long tranquillity. And go and tell them about that gospel, which, did the world embrace, it would never need another Waterloo."

Fain would we tell them; but in a short paper like this, we have only room for hints.

1. One most obvious advantage of peace is the occupation which it gives to industry. In time of war, markets are shut, and seas are dangerous. Looking on Britain as one huge factory — a factory which is willing to spin and weave for all the world, it is plain that a declaration of hostilities is the same thing as the closing of many mar-

9*

kets. Nations against whom Britain is in
arms, refuse to take her goods; and though
neutral or friendly nations may still be willing to take them, they can not so easily
get them. The path of the ocean is infested by privateers and ships-of-war; and
the expense of transport is terribly enhan-
ced by the augmented rates of insurance,
and by long detentions in waiting for a convoy; so that while the manufacturer loses
one customer by losing the hostile nation,
in consequence of the higher price of his
commodities, the customer whom he keeps
can only buy a smaller share. For instance, in the last year of the war, in 1814,
there were exported from this country six
thousand tons of hardware and cutlery;
but in ten years of peace, the quantity had
doubled, and in twenty years had nearly
trebled.* In 1801, there were consumed

* The exact numbers were:—

In 1814	.	.	.	.	6,162 tons.
" 1824	.	.	.	.	12,285 "
" 1834	.	.	.	.	16,275 "

Porter's "Progress of the Nation."

in the cotton manufactures of this empire about fifty millions of pounds of the raw material, and this quantity continued nearly stationary till the close of the war. But, five years after the restoration of peace, the consumption had trebled; in ten years it was quadruple; in twenty it had increased sixfold; and in thirty years, it was twelve times as great as it had been from the commencement to the close of hostilities.*

In other words, since peace was established, employment has multiplied three-fold or fourfold for the workmen of Birmingham and Sheffield; and for the spinners of Glasgow and Manchester, in a ratio of twelve to one.

2. And while the operatives of this coun-

---

* The consumption of cotton in the mills of Britain was as follows:—

1801	.	.	54,203,433 lbs.
1814	. . . .	.	53,777,802 "
1820	. . .	.	152,829,633 "
1825	. . .	.	202,546,809 "
1835	. . .	.	333,043,464 "
1845	. . .	.	592,581,600 "

The last year is derived from *Du Fay and Co.'s Trade Report;* the rest from Porter.

try have been thus contributing to the comfort of the human brotherhood, supplying scissors, knives, and fowling-pieces, to the Indian hunter and the African villager, and apparel to all the world, the recompense has come back into their own wardrobe and cupboard, and the modern mechanic has become a far wealthier man than his forefather was. The twenty million pounds' worth of cotton goods which we annually ship for other shores, and the corresponding productions of other sorts, return in commodities good for food and pleasant to the eye. And though an English laborer may earn no more shillings in a week than he could have earned thirty years ago, these shillings will procure comforts and accommodations now which they could not have compassed then. And I need not say that wealth lies not in the shilling, but in the shilling's worth—not in the quantity of coin which a man possesses, but in the amount of commodities which, at a given time and place, that coin will procure.

Applying this test of opulence, we may thankfully conclude, that amid all its remaining privations, British industry is better conditioned now than it has ever been; and we may trust that, with peace among the nations, and with sobriety and self-control among the citizens, the standard of comfort will steadily ascend.

To make the improvement palpable, we might appeal to the better clothing of the artisan and of his wife and children. And we might refer to the better furniture of his abode. But we select an instance in those articles which were once the luxury of the rich, but are now, to some extent, the privilege of all. In 1814, there were imported, for Britain's home consumption, 19,224,154 lbs. of tea. In 1846, the import had mounted to 47,500,000 lbs. That is, in the former year, each inhabitant of the United Kingdom consumed a pound of tea; in the latter year, there was an allowance to each of one pound ten ounces. In 1814, there were imported about 6,000,-

000 lbs. of coffee. In 1846, the import of coffee for domestic use had risen to 36,-781,391 lbs. That is, there was, in the former year, an allowance of five ounces, or thereby, and in the latter, nearly a pound and a quarter to each inhabitant of Great Britain and Ireland.* In 1814 there were imported 223,775,888 lbs. of sugar. In 1846 there were entered for consumption 547,292,816 lbs. That is, assuming the population of Great Britain and Ireland as eighteen millions at the former period and thirty millions at the latter, we have, at the earlier date, twelve pounds of sugar for each inhabitant, and at the later period, eighteen pounds.† And what renders this

---

* To which may be added 3,000,000 lbs. of cocoa in 1846 against nothing in 1814.

† The above calculations are founded on statements contained in the house of commons' report on commercial relations with China (1847); reports of meetings at Liverpool on the tea duties; M‘Culloch's Dictionary of Commerce; the last edition of the Encyclopædia Britannica; the trade circulars of Messrs, T. and H. Littledale, of Liverpool, and Messrs. Ripley, Brown, & Co., of London; along with items of information obligingly communicated by personal friends.

progress peculiarly cheering, is the assurance that it is mainly a progress among the working-classes. The wealthier members of the community consume no more at present than they did forty years ago, for even when the article was dearest they used as much as they required. Other people only use as much as they can afford; and though we wish they could afford a great deal more, we are glad to find that the mass of the population can now command these healthful and innocent enjoyments to an extent which no other nation knows, and which, to our frugal fathers would have looked like dangerous luxury.

3. But there is another way in which the commonwealth has profited by peace. It has let loose much of the capital, and all the mind and soul which were formerly locked up in the great business of fighting. By its constant demands, war drains the wealth of a kingdom, and instead of spending his money in building mills, or improving waste lands, the capitalist is obliged to

pay some of it into the exchequer in the shape of positive taxes, and is tempted to pay over the remainder in the shape of lucrative loans. And even though taxation did not rise, and though the capitalist continued as wealthy as before, war makes him timid and retentive ; afraid to launch a ship to-day which may be captured to-morrow ; afraid to build a factory this autumn, which the torch of the invader may reduce to ashes next spring ; afraid to commence some costly process of production, when the market for which he designed it may be shut in a moment, and remain hermetically closed for years to come. But encouraged by protracted peace, the capital of England has waxed courageous and confident, and has given to the workingmen of these kingdoms an extent and continuance of employment without a parallel in modern story.

.And peace has set free, for the purposes of human improvement, that large amount of intelligence which war, the monster-monopolist, absorbed into itself. In the fighting times the engineer exerted his skill to invent new implements of destruction, and was mighty in catamarans, and rocket-tubes, and martello-towers ; and incandescent with phosphorus and sulphur, the patriotic chymist exercised himself in cheapening gunpowder, and discovering Greek fire. The two ventricles of the nation's heart were the horse-guards and the admiralty, and all thought and interest, the nation's very life, flowed through them. And though sometimes a gentle spirit hinted a mitigation of the criminal code, or a concession to some overburdened class, the rebuffs which he perpetually encountered taught him that he was born before the time. But, when peace arrived, the volunteer beat his sword into a ploughshare, and the soldier became philanthropist. It was no longer needful for the mind of the nation to deposite its first-fruits on the altar of Moloch ; but, without impeachment of his loyalty, the mechanist, and statesman, and the lover of his species, might devote his energies to useful inventions and civic reforms, and all those benevolent labors which tend to make a bad world better.

We can not recount all the discoveries of this peaceful age, from a lucifer-match up to a railroad, and from a steamship down to a pair of gutta-percha goloshes. But these discoveries have made the modern laborer a mightier man than an ancient lord. Just look at your lot, and wonder at your wealth. There was your worthy father—when he wanted to be up betimes, he lost half the night listening to the village clock, and starting up at all the hours except the right one ; and when at last, a trifle late, he jumped out of bed, and got hold of the tinder-box, after ten minutes' practice with the flint and steel, heated but not enlightened, through sleet and slush he had to seek his neighbor's door, and borrow a burning brand. But soundly reposing all the night, and by an alarum roused at the appointed minute, you rasp the ready match

across the sanded surface, and turn the
stopcock of the magic tube, and in a moment are surrounded by an affluence of the
purest light. It was in the Brighton van
that your father travelled, that hard season
when he visited the coast in search of work,
and he never got the better of the long,
bleak journey. But for your own diversion
you took the trip the other day. You went
in the morning and returned at night, and it
cost you neither cough nor rheumatism,
and less money altogether than you would
have paid for one night's jolting in the frosty
van. When the last letter came from your
poor brother in the north — penny stamps
were not invented then — and you remember how rueful you felt, as the postman re-
fused to leave the precious packet, for you
had not in all the house a shilling and
threepence halfpenny. And when your
uncle broke his leg, and the bungling sur
geon set it so badly, that it had to be broken and set anew, after all his torture he
never got full use of it again. But when

you put out your shoulder-blade, you can not tell how they set it to rights; for all your remembrance is, the doctor holding some fragrant essence to your nostrils, and when you awoke from a pleasant trance, the arm was supple, and you yourself all straight and trim.

To peace we are indebted for cities lit with gas, and rivers alive with steam. To peace we owe the locomotive and the telegraph, which have made the British towns one capital, and remotest provinces the enclosing park. To peace our thanks are due for food without restriction, and intercourse without expense; for journeys without fatigue, and operations without pain; cheap correspondence and cheap corn; railway cars and chloroform. And to the same bounteous source—or rather to the Giver of peace, and of every perfect gift— we stand beholden for the hundred expedients which now combine to make life longer and more happy.

But far better than such material boons

are the social and moral blessings which
have followed in the train of peace. It
has given us leisure to review our position,
and has not only revealed, but remedied
some of its worst evils. It has enabled us
o emancipate our slaves, and it has short-
ened the hours of factory labor. It has
so enlarged the franchise that no frugal citizen need despair of attaining it; and it has
given to public opinion a legislative power
which it never knew before. It has revised
our criminal jurisprudence, and has ex-
punged from the statute-book the greater
number of its sanguinary laws. And it
has lately been turning a benevolent eye
toward the abodes and occupations of the
poor, and has sought to give the sons of
toil cheerful amusements and salubrious
dwellings. And by removing taxes on
knowledge, and by improvements in print-
ing, it has made the newspaper a familiar
visiter of cottages, and has rendered bibles
and other books as cheap as loaves of bread.

When the New Zealand chief was going

10*

to war, and the missionary remonstrated, he exclaimed : " But what shall I do with my barrels of gunpowder?" So might Britain have remonstrated, could any one have warned her that there was to be no more fighting for thirty successive years. " What will become of all our energies? our combativeness and enterprise, and love of adventure? and all the heroic ingredients of our national character? We must have a battle, though it were only to keep so much good gunpowder from spoiling." But God himself has found another outlet for these energies ; and it is with God's own enemy and man's—it is with moral evil—that the great battle is now begun. Fighting on the field of foreign heathenism and home-bred depravity, every teacher of a ragged school or a Sunday class, every faithful superintendent of a penitentiary or a convict-ship, and every earnest minister or missionary is a soldier ; and every outcast reclaimed, every child instructed, and every human being won

over to the cause of piety and virtue, is
another victory. This is the great contest
of our age; and in this bloodless battle we
long to see enlisted all the chivalry and
prowess of our Anglo-Saxon world. We
long to see a holy war in which men shall
fight with their own bad passions, and shall
seek to demolish nothing, except those
works of the devil which the Son of God
came to destroy. We long to see a cam-
paign, not of race against race, nor of class
against class; but a crusade of all races
and all classes against whatever is ungodly
and selfish here below. We long to
see—precursor of the Prince of peace—
a war in which the Bible shall be the
standard, and Christianity the uniform; in
which the gospel or love divine shall be the
only weapon, and sin the only enemy; a war
in which the watchword and the rallying
cry shall be, " Glory to God in the highest;
on earth peace, good-will toward man."*

* To show how extensively the evangelical spirit has
spread, and how greatly Christian philanthropy has

And now that it is done, do you ask the purpose of this paper? It is, first of all, to make the reader and the writer thankful. It is, to make more vivid to our minds God's goodness in casting our lot on this tranquil time.

strengthened during these peaceful years, we might refer to the statistics of any religious society. For instance, in 1814, the Bible society had a revenue of 87,216*l.*, and issued 352,569 copies of the Scriptures; but in the year ending March, 1847, its income was 117,440*l.*, and its issues were 1,419,283 copies. And the following table, from returns kindly furnished by the secretaries, shows the relative income and missionary staff of the four leading societies:—

	INCOME.		NUMBER OF MISSIONARIES.	
	1814.	1847.	1814.	1847.
Church of England	10,788*l.*	101,294*l.*	22	180*a.*
Wesleyan ..	9,554	103,619	70	411
London . . .	19,429	76,319	68	165*b*
Baptist. . . .	7,000	25,000	20	70*c*

To which may be added the many societies which had no existence at the earlier period. It is only five years since the Free Church of Scotland became a distinct community, and in that time it has contributed for Christian purposes upward of a million and a half of money.

a Besides 1298 country-born and native teachers.
b Besides 700 teachers.
c Besides 159 teachers.

And we have written with a view to per-
petuate the blessing. We confess a desire
for the spread of pacific principles; and
we would urge their importance on that
class of the community who, if not the
greatest gainers in peace, are the first and
the sorest sufferers in war.

But what can a working man contribute
toward the grand result of "peace on
earth"? He can contribute to society one
peaceful citizen. Forming his own opinions and holding his own convictions, he can
lay down and carry out the rule of leaving
truth to fight its own battle. He can foster
in his children habits of magnanimity and
mutual forbearance, and can teach them tha
" greater is he who ruleth his spirit than he
who taketh a city." He can exhibit that
brightest heroism which retaliates evil with
good ; and he may do his endeavor to spread
that gospel which is the grand peace-
maker. And looking forward to the day
when the weapons of the warrior, like the
engines of the inquisitor, shall only survive

on the shelves of the museum, as relics of a
fearful barbarism, he may even now, by his
practical suffrage, recognise the majesty of
mind and the meanness of physical force.

And he can teach his fellow-workmen
the more excellent way for obtaining their
just demands. Break the head of a bur-
gess or yeoman, and however liberal his
former leanings, you make him at once an
enemy of the popular cause; burn a cot-
ton-mill, and, by raising the rates of insurance and ruining confidence — confidence
in the good-sense and forbearance of the
English people — you make the owner hesitate whether he will build another; burn a
second, and the owner does not hesitate,
but at once withdraws to safer regions his
capital and his family, and leaves to lasting
misery some hundreds of your fellows;
burn a dozen, and Lancashire will soon be
a Saxon Tipperary, with no smoking chimneys to deface the landscape, nor any factory bell to disturb the ragged holyday; but,
unlike the Celtic Tipperary, without a mar-

ket for its pigs, and when potatoes rot, without a hard-working neighbor to send it beef and bread. But let the industrious classes advance in education and principle, and there is no political privilege which they need despair of attaining, nor any which a right-hearted citizen would grudge to share with them. The working-classes will find their most eloquent argument, as well as their most effective armor, in their own worth and intelligence.

And every laborer who, in the manifesto of Messiah the prince, has read that golden sentence, " Blessed are the peacemakers, for they shall be called the children of God," may pray, " O, Prince of peace, thy kingdom come — thy kingdom of righteousness, and peace, and joy." He may pray for the quick arrival of that time when, beneath the Saviour's benignant sceptre, the Bible shall supplant the baton, and the gospel shall silence the gun; and joined in cordial brotherhood, the sons of Adam shall again behold this earth a happy home!

THE OASIS.

THE sabbath is God's gracious present to a working world; and for wearied minds and bodies it is the grand restorative. The Creator has given us a natural restorative — sleep; and a moral restorative — sabbath-keeping; and it is ruin to dispense with either. Under the pressure of high excitement, individuals have passed weeks together with little sleep, or none; but when the process is long-continued, the over-driven powers rebel, and fever, delirium, and death, come on. Nor can the natural amount be regularly curtailed without corresponding mischief. The sabbath does not arrive like sleep. The day of rest does not steal over us like the hour of slumber. It does not entrance us whether we will or not; but addressing us as intelligent beings, our Creator assures us that we need it, and bids us

notice its return, and court its renovation.
And if, rushing in the face of our Creator's
kindness, we force ourselves to work all
days alike, it is not long till we pay the for-
feit. The mental worker—the man of business or the man of letters—finds his ideas
coming turbid and slow; the equipoise of
his faculties is upset; he grows moody, fitful, and capricious; and with his mental
elasticity broken, should any disaster occur,
he subsides into habitual melancholy, or in
self-destruction speeds his guilty exit from
a gloomy world. And the manual worker
—the artisan, the engineer—fagging on
from day to day, and week to week, the
bright intuition of his eye gets blunted, and,
forgetful of their cunning, his fingers no
longer perform their feats of twinkling agil-
ity, nor, by a plastic and tuneful touch,
mould dead matter, or wield mechanic power; but, mingling his life's blood in his daily
drudgery, his locks are prematurely gray,
his genial humor sours, and, slaving it till
he has become a morose or reckless man,

for any extra effort, or any blink of balmy
feeling, he must stand indebted to opium or
alcohol. To an industrious population so
essential is the periodic rest, that when, in
France, the attempt was made to abolish
the weekly sabbath, it was found necessary
to issue a decree, suspending labor one day
in every ten. And in our own country, when
at attempt was made, in time of war, to work
a royal manufactory without a pause—at
the end of a few months, it was ascertained
that the largest amount of work had been
accomplished by the hands exempted from
Sunday labor.* Master manufacturers have
stated that they could perceive an evident

---

* "Not many years ago, a contractor went on to the
west with his hired men and teams to make a turnpike
road. At first he paid no regard to the sabbath ; but
continued his work as on other days. He soon found,
however, that the ordinances of nature, no less than the
moral law, were against him. His laborers became
sickly, his teams grew poor and feeble, and he was fully
convinced that more was lost than gained by working
on the Lord's day. So true is it that the sabbath-day
laborer, like the glutton and the drunkard, undermines
his health, and prematurely hastens the infirmities of
age, and his exit from the world."—*Dr. Humphrey of
America.*

deterioration in the quality of the goods produced as the week drew near a close, just because the tact, alertness, and energy of the workers began to experience inevitable exhaustion. When a steamer on the Thames blew up, not long ago, the firemen and stokers laid the blame on their broken sabbath· it stupified and embittered them—made them blunder at their work, and heedless what havoc these blunders might create. And we have been informed that, when the engines of an extensive steam-packet company in the south of England were getting constantly damaged, the mischief was instantly repaired by giving the men, what the bounty of their Creator had given them long before, the rest of each seventh day. And what is so essential to industrial efficiency, is no less indispensable to the laborer's health and longevity. This was well explained before a committee of the house of commons by an accomplished physician, Dr. Farre :—

"Although the night apparently equalizes

the circulation well, yet it does not sufficiently restore its balance for the attainment
of a *long* life. Hence one day in seven,
by the bounty of Providence, is thrown in
as a day of compensation, to perfect by its
repose the animal system. You may easily
determine this question as a matter of fact,
by trying it on beasts of burden. Take that
fine animal the horse, and work him to the
full extent of his powers every day of the
week, or give him rest one day in seven,
and you will soon perceive, by the superior
vigor, with which he performs his functions
on the other six days, that this rest is necessary to his well-being. Man, possessing a
superior nature, is borne along by the very
vigor of his mind, so that the injury of *continued* diurnal exertion and excitement on
his animal system is not so immediately apparent as it is in the brute; but, in the long
run, he breaks down more suddenly: it
abridges the length of his life and that
vigor of his old age, which (as to mere animal power) ought to be the object of his

preservation. * * * This is said simply as a physician, and without reference at all to the theological question ; but if you consider further the proper effect of real Christianity, namely, peace of mind, confiding trust in God, and goodwill to man, you will perceive in this source of renewed vigor to the mind, and through the mind to the body, an additional spring of life imparted from this higher use of the sabbath as a holy rest."

The sabbath is God's special present to the working man, and one chief object is to prolong his life and preserve efficient his working tone. In the vital system it acts like a compensation-pond : it replenishes the spirits, the elasticity, and vigor, which the last six days have drained away, and supplies the force which is to fill the six days succeeding. And in the economy of existence it answers the same purpose as, in the economy of income, is answered by a savings' bank. The frugal man who puts aside a pound to-day, and another pound

11*

next month, and who in a quiet way is always putting past his stated pound from time to time, when he grows old and frail gets not only the same pounds back again, but a good many pounds besides. And the conscientious man who husband's one day of existence every week — who, instead of allowing the sabbath to be trampled and torn in the hurry and scramble of life, treasures it devoutly up — the Lord of the sabbath keeps it for him, and in length of days and a hale old age gives it back with usury. The saving's bank of human existence is the weekly sabbath-day.

Another purpose for which the Father of earth's families has presented the workman with this day, is to enhance his domestic comfort and make him happy in his home. If it were not for this beneficent arrangement, many a toiling man would scarcely ever know the gentle glories and sweet endearments of his own fireside. Idle people are sometimes surfeited with the society of one another, and wealthy

people, however busy, can buy an occasional holyday. But though the working-man
gets from his employer only one or two days
of pastime in all the year, his God has given
him two-and-fifty sabbaths; and it is these
sabbaths which impart the sanctity and sweetness to the poor man's home. If he has
finished his marketing, and cleared off his
secular engagements on Saturday night, it
is marvellous what a look of leisure and
bright welcome ushers in the morrow, and
what a spirit of serene expectancy breathes
through the tidy and well-trimmed chamber. The peace of God lights up the pious laborer's dwelling, and, reserved from
a toil-worn week, the radiance of true love
pours freely forth in these gleams of sabbath sunshine. With graceful tint it touch-
es the deal chairs and homely table, and
converts a fathom of gray carpet into "a
wonder of the loom." It plays iridescent
among the quaint ornaments of the mantel-
shelf, streams over the hearth-stone, and
perches on the eight-day clock — the St.

Elm of rough weather past—the omen of
good days to come. It penetrates affectionate bosoms, and revives old memories
deep and tender, which, but for such weekly resurrection, might have died for ever;
and with early interest and endearment it
suffuses that face which on sabbath morns
is always young, and reminds the proud
possessor of that wealth of quiet wisdom and
thoughtful kindness with which the Lord
has blessed his lot. And in the thaw of
friendly and thankful feelings, in the flow
of emotions cordial and devout, silent praises
sparkle in the eye, and the husband's love
and the father's joy well up to the very
brim.

"Hail, sabbath! thee I hail, the poor man's day:
  On other days the man of toil is doomed
  To eat his joyless bread, lonely; the ground
  Both seat and board, screened from the winter's cold
  And summer's heat by neighboring hedge or tree.
  But on this day, embosomed in his home,
  He shares the frugal meal with those he loves;
  With those he loves he shares the heartfelt joy
  Of giving thanks to God."

But beyond all these, God's gift of the sabbath should be precious to the working world as its main opportunity for moral and spiritual improvement, and as its best preparative for a happy immortality. While eternity is hastening apace, the exigencies of each successive moment are banishing the thought of it, and many are surprised into the great hereafter before they have distinctly perceived that themselves are on the road to it. The sabbath brings a weekly pause, and in its own mild but earnest accents says to each, Whither art thou going? while its benignant hours invite the pilgrim of earth to that better country of which it is at once the angel and the specimen. The sabbath brings leisure; it gives a day for thinking ; and it brings seclusion. From the daily vortex — from the crowd so dizzy and profane, it snatches the whirling waif — it pulls him aside into its little sanctuary, and leaves him alone with God On the table of the busy man, whether rich or poor, it spreads the open Bible, and

wakes again the oracle which has spoken
the saving word to thousands. To the intent and adoring eye it unveils that wondrous
cross where redemption was achieved and
God was reconciled; and by the vista of
one radiant tomb it guides the musing spirit
far beyond the land of graves; while per-
fumed gales and Eolian pulses from its
opened window bespeak the nearer heaven,
and stir the soul wirh immortality. To the
man who has got the sabbatic sentiment—
to the man who has received from above
the spiritual instinct, what a baptism of
strength and joy does the Lord's day bring!
From prayerful slumber he wakes amid its
gentle light, and finds it spreading round
him like a balm. There are hope and comfort in its greeting, and from prayerful retirement he joins his family circle with peace
in his conscience and freshness in all his
feelings. The books which he reads, and
the truths which he hears, expand his intellect, and fill it with thoughts noble, pure,
and heavenly   The public worship gives

rise, and by giving outlet, gives increase to hallowed emotions and Christian affections. The psalmody awakens gratitude, cheerfulness, and praise; and the comprehensive prayers and confessions remind him of evils which he himself has overlooked, and perils and temptations of which he was not aware. Interceding for others, his soul dilates in sympathy and public spirit. Friends vaguely remembered — friends long parted or on foreign shores, and on bustling days wellnigh forgotten — now join his earnest fellowship; and prayer hallows while it deepens ancient amity. The poor, the sick, the broken-hearted, prisoners, slaves, the whole family of sorrow, flit before the suppliant's eye and leave him with a softer heart. And the realm and its rulers recur at this sacred moment, and every sentiment is merged in loyalty and Christian patriotism. And the heralds of salvation, pastors, teachers, missionaries, with all the evangelistic agency, are recalled to mind, and while his interest in Christ's cause becomes more

personal, his soul expands in catholicity.
And, if in a willing mood, from the word
read and expounded, he carries home en-
lightenment, invigoration, impulse; and with
big emotions, and blessed hopes, the sabbath sends him forth on a busy week and a
restless world, a tranquil presence and an
elevating power.*

To cross an eastern desert is often arduous work.   And as they jog on their grunt-
ing asses, or swing on their melancholy
camels, — as the sun pours his downright
embers, and shadows are projected short
and round, — as the water-bags grow empty,
and, for lack of pomegranate or citron, each
squeezes in his cheek the juiciest pebble
he can find, the travellers are apt to droop
into a moody silence, and lose all liking
for their journey.   With dust in every pore,
and fever in every vein, nobody cares for
his neighbor, nor feels the slightest interest
in any earthly thing.   And should some

* The foregoing paragraphs appeared in the *North
British Review* for May, 1848.

THE OASIS.

sprightly comrade still hold out, his wit is
resented as rudeness, and he himself is
hated for his irksome glee. But presently
they glimpse the green banner in the distant sky, the palm-signal which tells of
water, and verdure, and repose. And as
they reach the leafy tent, and fling themselves on the cool ground, and climb for
the date-clusters, and through the sandy
filter scoop the hidden fountain, their soul
is restored, and their interest in all things
revives. Wife and children are dear again,
and home is much desired; and as the artist points his pencil, and the scholar takes
out his book, the caravan dissolves in
friendly talk and flowing soul. And, reader,
like that desert route, your daily toil is a
life-wasting drudgery. Resumed morning
by morning, and followed hour by hour, it
drains the strength and dries the soul. But
at the end of every weekly march, behold
yon green OASIS! Like palm-tree shadow,
behold the welcome which the rest-day
waves! And as it bids you eat and drink

12

abundantly, do you obey the genial sign.
Turn in to tarry beneath the refreshful
canopy, and you will find the recompense
in a replenished heart and a renovated
home; and as, full of heaven's peace and
strength, you issue from its sweet asylum,
you will resume life's journey rejoicing.

But though we have mentioned the uses
of the sabbath first, we must not forget its
obligation. If you have got a healthy
mind — one conscientious, and dutiful, and
right with God — your main question will
ever be, not, What is for my interest? but
what is right? what would God have me
to do? You will have no fear but that
duty and interest will in the long run coin-
cide; still, you will perceive a positive and
immediate pleasure in obedience; it will be
your meat and drink to do the will of your
Father in heaven. And on this subject,
the will of God is plain and peremptory.
As early as the creation of the human race,
he showed his purpose regarding the sabbath. "On the seventh day, God ended

his work which he had made; and he
rested on the seventh day from all his work
which he had made; and God blessed the
seventh day, and sanctified it; because
that in it he had rested from all his work
which God created and made." And accordingly, when, in all the pomp of Mount
Sinai, that moral law was given which has
ever since been the great standard of right
and wrong, the fourth of the ten commandments was, "Remember the sabbath-day,
to keep it holy. Six days shalt thou labor
and do all thy work; but the seventh day
is the sabbath of the Lord thy God: in it
thou shalt not do any work, thou, nor thy
son, nor thy daughter, thy man-servant, nor
thy maid-servant, nor thy cattle, nor the
stranger that is within thy gates. For in six
days the Lord made heaven and earth, the
sea, and all that in them is, and rested the
seventh day: wherefore the Lord blessed
the sabbath-day and hallowed it. And all
through, from the first book of the Bible to
the last, we find the primeval blessing still

following the day, and the people of God devoutly keeping it. And perhaps there is no command which a special Providence has more signally guarded — none, the observance of which God has crowned with a more abundant recompense — and none of which the violation has been followed by a swifter or sorer frown. The will of God is clear; the command is plain and full; and it is not easy to estimate his guilt who tramples under foot an institution clothed with such divine authority, and fraught with such divine benignity.

And now the question comes round, how are we to spend the day so as to fulfil its Author's gracious purposes?

Among sabbatic employments, the most obvious is the public and private worship of God. On other days you have little time for meditation and prayer; but on a sabbath morning you have leisure. Take your bible, read a portion, and think over it. In prayer, try to remember the sins and errors of the week, and ask pardon for

the Saviour's sake; and try to recall your
recent mercies, and, as you reckon them
one by one, bless the Lord for his benefits.
And consider what farther blessings you
stand in need of, and with humble earnestness implore them from that munificent
Giver who bestows so bounteously, and
" who upbraideth not." And if you have
a household, let prayer and a passage of
God's word begin your family day; and
then let all resort to the house of God together; and when there, not only should
you listen to the messages and lessons
which God's minister brings you, but seek
to put your whole heart into the services
of prayer and praise. The thing which
has made you sometimes feel dull in a
place of worship, was, that you did not
worship. Your body was there, but your
mind was everywhere. Pray that God
would fix your thoughts; and if you be
all *ear* when the chapter is read and the
sermon preached, all *voice* when the psalms
are sung, and all *heart* when the prayers

are offered, yov will not weary at the time
and the hallowed effect will follow you
home.

A great help toward spending the Lord's
day rightly is a well-selected library. From
a friend you may borrow a good book, now
and then ; but it is desirable to have a little
stock of your own. It would be a great
matter if you could compass a book like
" Henry's Commentary," or the commentary published by the Tract society; for,
besides throwing great light on the Bible,
it would furnish you with endless Sunday
reading. And if you wish to get solid
and extensive acquaintance with sacred
truth, you can not do better than master
" Dwight's System of Theology." We
have known working men who did so.
Books like the " Pilgrim's Progress," and
" D'Aubigne's History of the Reforma-
tion," the Lives of Henry Martyn, and
John Newton, and Colonel Gardiner,
' Abbott's Young Christian," " Williams's
Missionary Enterprise in the South Seas,'

and "Moffat's Labors in Africa,"—such
books would be interesting to the young
folk, as well as instructive to yourself.
And it would be well to possess and read
prayerfully such books as "Pike's Persua-
sives to Early Piety," and "James's Anxious Inquirer," and "Baxter's Saint's
Everlasting Rest." All these books have
been published in cheap forms; and in
shops where they sell books second-hand,
you may get the largest of them for very
little money. And the man who has such
companions in his house, and who has any
real earnestness about his immortal soul,
will find ways and means to spend profit-
ably each returning sabbath.

And in order to make it a cheerful day
to your children, you would do well to
enter zealously into their sabbath employments. It is likely that you send them to
the Sunday-school; but the punctuality
with which they attend, and the proficiency
which they exhibit there, depend very much
on their parents. If you invite them to

repeat to you their hymns and other lessons — and if they find that diligence is rewarded, not only by a teacher's love, but by a father's smile — they will ply their tasks with new vivacity. And, as a reward of good conduct, you might read over to them, or allow them to read to you, one of the little books they bring home. Children are, in general, fond of music; and you might sometimes spend half an hour very sweetly in singing psalms or hymns together.

Addressing our industrious fellow-citizens, we can not close without warning them against a twofold jeopardy, which presently threatens the day marked off by God for the laborer's leisure. There is an attempt on the part of some wealthy men to buy up the sabbath of the poor, and there is a tendency on the part of some working men to pilfer the sabbath of their fellow-workmen. Rich men, hasting to become still richer, are anxious to receive their letters on the Lord's day; and in

order to save time for business, they wish
to perform their journeys on that day; and
to increase the profits of their investments
in railways, and steamers, and tea-gardens,
and rural taverns, they are anxious to create
among the working classes a taste for Sunday trips and pleasure parties. They bribe
the engineer and the letter-carrier; and,
for the rich man's money, these workmen
barter their sabbath; and they tempt the
town artisan and the city shopman, and,
for the sake of the cheap excursion or the
merry ploy, the artisan and shopman are
enticed to squander both their money and
their souls.

On the other hand, from improvidence,
or indolence, or some other cause, the sabbath morning finds many working people
with no food in their houses, and, going
out to purchase it, they compel their fellow-workmen — the grocers, and butchers,
and bakers, and their assistants — to toil in
their service half the sabbath-day; while
other workmen hie away to the river or the

railway station, and compel another class
of their fellow-workmen — sailors, and en-
gine-drivers, and waiters in taverns — to
toil till midnight in supplying them with
pleasure.   And in this way, in the capital
of the kingdom, there are 20,000 people
working in shops, and at least as many
more connected with public conveyances
and places of public entertainment, who
never know a sabbath.   And where are
the robbers who have wrenched from these
British citizens their birthright of a weekly
repose?   Who are the tyrants who thus
grind the faces of the poor?   We grieve to
    swer — poor men — working men.

Now, recollecting that the sabbath is the
poor man's day — that it is the providen-
tial bulwark against over-production and
under-payment — that it is the grand restorative of the laborer's wasted strength and
spirits, and the reviver of his domestic
joys — that it is, in short, the palladium of
his present and eternal happiness, — and
recollecting, farther, that if the poor lend it

to one another, they must soon sell it to
the rich, and by-and-by do seven days'
work for the six days' pay, — we put it to
yourselves, if the workman who makes a
merchandise of his sabbath is not a traitor
to his class? And, leaving religious con-
siderations out of view, we ask if the laborer
who spurns the filthy lucre offered for his
sabbath hours, and who, perhaps, sacrifices
a good situation over and above — we ask,
if, instead of being jeered for his scruples,
he does not deserve the thanks of all his
fellows, as the Hampden or the Tell of
industrial freedom?

So far as the Sunday excursion goes, the
workman forfeits little who does without it.
"As it is not all gold that glitters, neither
is it all true pleasure that usurps the name.
There is a way which seemeth right unto
a man, but the end thereof are the ways
of death. Even in laughter the heart is
sorrowful, and the end of that mirth is
heaviness. Never shall I forget the mourn-
ful accents with which a condemned crim-

inal, shortly before he was executed, said in my hearing, that his crimes began with small thefts and pleasure excursions on the Lord's day."* To us, no excursion is pleasure which is not pleasant when ended. But in what does the pleasure of the Sunday ploy consist next morning? Is it in the choice friendships you have made, or the sum which you have added to your savings? Is it in the additional energy which bulges in your muscles, and the limpid clearness with which the stream of thought and feeling flows? Or is it in the great calm which fills your conscience — the happy thought how much you have done for God and for your fellow-men? Or is it in the unwonted neatness with which your habitation smiles on your return, and the fresh alacrity with which you resume the morrow's task? "I lodged," says a shrewd observer, "within a stone-cast of the great Manchester and Birmingham rail-

* Dr. King's Words to the Working Classes on the Sabbath Question.

way. I could hear the roaring of the trains along the line, from morning till near mid-day, and during the whole afternoon ; and, just as the evening was setting in, I saun-tered down to the gate by which a return train was discharging its hundreds of pas sengers, fresh from the sabbath amusements of the country, that I might see how they looked. There did not seem much of enjoyment about the wearied and some-what draggled groups : they wore, on the contrary, rather an unhappy physiognomy, as if they had missed spending the day quite to their minds, and were now return ing, sad and disappointed, to the round of toil from which it ought to have proved a sweet interval of relief. A congregation just dismissed from hearing a vigorous dis-course, would have borne, to a certainty, a more cheerful air."*

Our reader has likely tried the plan of Sunday diversions already. Have they made you a healthier or a happier man?

* Hugh Miller's First Impressions of England.

Have they made you richer, or a **more** respected member of society? Or have they not consumed a large amount of your hard-won earnings, and often sent you to Monday's toils more weary than you left them on Saturday night? Have they not involved you with worthless and abandoned acquaintances, and sometimes left on your mind a gloomy foreboding and a guilty fear? And do you never tremble to think what the end of these things must be? Many a Sunday trip has had for its terminus the jail, the convict-ship, the scaffold. Many a broken sabbath has been the first step in a career which ended in drunkenness, in theft, in murder. And every sabbath-breaker is going forward to the bar of God. Dear reader, accept as a timely message these friendly lines. Seek pardon for the past, and, in the Lord's strength, make trial of the better way. For the sake of a peaceful conscience, for the sake of a prosperous week, for the sake of a happy home, for the sake of an approving God,

"Remember the sabbath-day, to keep it holy;" and you will shortly prove the truth of the promise, " If thou turn away thy foot from the sabbath, from doing thy pleasure on my holy day, and call the sabbath a delight, the holy of the Lord, honorable ; and shalt honor him, not doing thine own ways, nor finding thine own pleasure, nor speaking thine own words: then shalt thou delight thyself in the Lord, and I will cause thee to ride upon the high places of the earth, and feed thee with the heritage of Jacob, thy father; for the mouth of the Lord hath spoken it."

THE FIRESIDE.

In Southern Europe they have no house-hold fires; but when there is snow on the mountains, or ice in the wind, they get a chafing-dish, and comfort their toes with glowing charcoal. And in Russia and the north, so fiercely blows the winter-blast, that they are fain to defend themselves from behind an intrenchment of flues, and stoves, and fire-clay furnaces. And it is only our own happy clime, so crisp in the morning, and so mild at the winter-noon, which rejoices in that glorious institution, the open hearth and blazing ingle.

As to the fuel or the style of the fire-place, we have no sectarian feeling. The old English method is to adjust in a vast chimney a log of pine, with a few support-ing fagots; and as the flame leaps, and roars, and crackles on a clear night in some

lofty banquet-hall, it makes a right baronial
blaze. In as far as it needs no grate, this
plan is rather economical; but as it also
needs a grand mansion, with turrets on the
top and an ancient forest round it, the
saving is somewhat counterbalanced. And
a good fire may be made by flanking a few
peats with a lump of coke or anthracite;
and if it be Wales or the Highlands, and
if there be rime on the ground and frozen
rooks on the tree, the blue smoke is beautiful, and the turfy odor delicious. But for
us in London, where peats are as dear as
penny loaves, it is a great satisfaction to
know that they yield a profusion of dust.
It was a "bonny" fire to which King James
treated his wealthy subject, George Heriot;
and still "bonnier," in the eyes of a needy
prince, was the fire with which the gold-
smith repaid his hospitality, next morning,
when he fed the flame, not with billets of
cedar, but with the king's "promises to
pay." And very beautiful is the mountain
of blazing splints, with a torch of candle-

13*

coal in the front of them,—like the mir-
rored sun in a golden temple of Peru—
such as may be seen in Lanarkshire or
Durham, or some other igneous paradise,
flinging through all the recesses of a mighty
farm-kitchen its wealth of revealing flame.
But bonfires like these are beyond the
reach of authors and readers on the banks
of the Thames; and therefore we set down
a recipe which our wife acquired from our
younger brother, and which we have often
found very seductive about ten o'clock at
night :—

    " Take three or four fragments of walls-
end; lay them together; and when thoroughly lighted, take the tongs, and place
tenderly over them all the large cinders
from under the grate; and then over the
cinders, and layer by layer, shovel every
particle of ashes, as carefully as if it were
diamond dust; and in half an hour the
skilful concrete will be one huge and
ardent ruby. Then talk, read or darn
stockings; and wonder which is happiest,

you or the queen." Besides greatly lightening the dustman's labors next morning, this device will be found a great saving of fuel.

And as for the fireplace, please yourselves. We have never seen any which we liked so well as the Carron grate in our own nursery, some ages agone. On either panel a cast-metal shepherd played on a cast-metal pipe; and on the shining hob there often simmered a few prunes or a honey posset, which a kind-hearted aunt had provided for our frequent colds; and in some retreat below it a mouse had found a cozy hermitage, and every time that they stirred the fire the mouse came out, and then ran back again as soon as the pother was over. We often wonder what has become of the grate and the mouse: we know too well what has become of the nursery.

But, after all, the charm of an English hearth is neither polished bars nor blazing brands, but the true and loving faces which it shines upon. Its charm is the conjugal affection, the parental hope, the filial piety, the neighborly good-will, which cluster round it and form **THE FIRESIDE.**

Judging, however, by hints which we have occasionally received — chiefly from our lady readers — there is room for improvement in many of the "Homes of England." We will not betake ourselves to the indolent subterfuge of saying that there are faults on either side; but shall let our fair correspondents speak for themselves, and shall then offer a few suggestions for the good of our readers in general.

"TO MR. HAPPY HOME.

"SIR: If you wish your paper to be of any use, you must come nearer the point. Hitherto I consider it a perfect failure, and without it improves very much I shall give up taking it in. I wish you would speak to my husband. Tell him that a woman can no. always be cleaning of a house, if as soon as the mop is out of her hand, a great boor comes tramping up stairs, with all Holborn sticking to his heels. Tell him that it is time for him to be doing something better for his family. I have heard of bricklayers who became master-builders in no time; and I certainly did not expect that my husband should be wearing a leather apron up to this precious time of day. And if he does not wish me to become a perfect fright, tell him to get me a new bonnet.

"I am, yours, &c.,

"CATHARINA CRUMPET CAYENNE."

"SIR, my husband Is a bruit. he keps a keb. he takes car to feed his horse, and to get a good diner for himself, but he leaves me Without enuf to by a morsle. now, sir, i takes verry bad with this, for i been a Cook and always yused to my wittles kumfortabal Before i marry this Great bear.

"BETSEY CAPERS."

"Sir: Five years ago I was one of the happiest women in England, for I was then united to one who loved me, and of whose affection I was proud. And though I know that I was very imperfect, yet, for Robert's sake, I was constantly striving to improve. It was all my pleasure to hear St. Pancras strike six, for then I knew that a few minutes would bring him home, and the room would be tidy, and the kettle would be singing, and something would be ready for Robert to look at, or something that needed his help before it could be finished. And he was always so handy: in those evening hours he made the cradle for our little boy, and a green-painted Venetian to keep out the sun at our southern window. And many a beautiful book have we gone through, reading it aloud by turns. But, for a good while past, a change has come over my dear husband. He has not taken to drinking, or anything really bad; but he has got so fond of politics. He is a fine scholar and an orator; and at first I was vain to think that the club could not do without him. But I must now confess, sir, that it takes up all his thoughts. He has not the same spirit for his work, and I have very little of his company. Last night he came in for his tea in a sad hurry, and swallowed it without speaking a word, for he was engaged to one of these meetings. And I fear that I looked cross, for, as he put on his hat, he spoke to me in a way that my Robert never spoke to me before. Tell him, dear sir, that I was not sulking: I was thinking of our happy evenings, and how he might now be giving a lesson to our little George. And tell him, that if he will only give his wife some of those sweet hours he did not use to grudge, she will strive to deserve them better. I am not clever enough to understand, as he does, the affairs of the nation, but I quite agree with him in wishing all to be free and happy.

"Excuse me for not giving my name; but allow me to subscribe myself, yours respectfully,   "A KEEPER AT HOME."

It is the difficult task of the workman's wife to make the fireside an attractive and improving place—a place round which husbands and sons will be glad to gather when the work of the day is done. And in attempting this, you may possibly find assistance in the following hints :—

1. *Be tidy.*—Some wives, who are sufficiently industrious, have no talent for neatness. They are constantly scrubbing and scouring, and they keep chairs and tables marching and counter-marching from one apartment to another; but, except the turmoil at the time, and the humid exhalations afterward, there are no products of their ill-directed energy; in a day or two, all is the same dirt and disorder as ever. Others, you do not know when their house-cleaning is done, for you never find them worried and in dishabille; but, somehow, their furniture always finds its proper place; their hearth is always bright, and a limpid daylight always looks in at their unsullied window.

Few things are more apt to send a man to the playhouse or tavern, than a filthy or uproarious fireside. When he comes home in the evening, and finds his apartment a chaos of frowzy garments, and broken dishes, and potato parings, and squalling children; or a laundry steaming with wet linen, and fragrant with soap-suds, he is very apt to light his pipe and sally forth in search of a more cheerful scene. And, therefore, every woman who would save her husband from the gin-shop and bad company, should contrive to get all her bustle and rough work completed betimes, and have a trim and smiling chamber awaiting his return.*

2. *Be thrifty.*—The picture of an industrious and frugal housewife was sketched

* There are now wash-houses provided in many places, where, for a payment of twopence or threepence, an active woman may do all the washing of an ordinary family in a few hours. Hot water, drying apparatus, smoothing irons, and a mangle are provided ; and besides all the economy of time and money, the linen is dried without being soiled, and your own abode is saved the horrors of the weekly ablution.

by an inspired pencil long ago, and many a Scotch and English matron might be quoted who has gone far to repeat the original. " Who can find a virtuous woman? for her price is far above rubies. The heart of her husband doth safely trust in her, so that he shall have no need of spoil. She seeketh wool and flax, and worketh willingly with her hands. She girdeth her loins with strength, and strengtheneth her arms. She layeth her hands to the spindle, and her hands hold the distaff. She is not afraid of the snow for her household; for all her household are doubly clothed. Her husband is known in the gates, when he sitteth among the elders of the land. She openeth her mouth with wisdom; and in her tongue is the law of kindness. She looketh well to the ways of her household, and eateth not the bread of idleness. Her children arise up and call her blessed; her husband also, and he praiseth her. Many daughters have done virtuously, but thou excellest them all. Favor is deceitful, and beauty is vain; but a woman that feareth the Lord she shall be praised."*

A man may work ever so hard; but, if his wife be not a good manager, no money will preserve his children from rags, nor his abode from wretchedness. And if, after all his earnings, he comes home to a joyless lodging; if, before he can obtain his supper, he has to go in search of his gossiping helpmeet, and by the way picks from the gutter his tattered son and heir; if he finds that his wife is too fine a lady to handle the broom or the needle; if he is ashamed when a neighbor drops in, or if, for want of a timely stitch, he himself can scarcely venture out, he is sure to grow abject or broken-hearted. He perceives that it is of little moment whether, at the end of the week, he brings home half-a-sovereign or half-a-crown, and sees no use in procuring gay dresses and bright ribands, which only render more grotesque the scare-crows around him. On the other hand, he must

* Proverbs xxxi.

be a mean-spirited mortal who can see the wife of his youth toiling and striving to se cure respectability and comfort for himself and his household, without straining his every nerve to help her. A savage may be content to bask in the sunshine, and look on while the mother of his children is catching fish or planting yams; but in England we trust there are few of these lazy churls. And we have known of instances not a few where a man has been reclaimed from idle or self-indulgent habits by the influence of a judicious and warm-hearted wife. The following is an instance, which we the more gladly give, because it occurred in the sister isle :—

"One day," says Mrs. Hall, "we entered a cottage in the suburbs of Cork: a young woman was knitting stockings at the door. It was as neat and comfortable as any in the most prosperous districts of England. We tell her brief story in her own words, as nearly as we can recall them:

"'My husband is a wheelwright, and

always earns his guinea a week; he was a good workman, but the love of drink was so strong in him, and it wasn't often he brought me more than five shillings out of his one pound on a Saturday night, and it broke my heart to see the children too ragged to send to school, to say nothing of the starved look they had, out of the little I could give them. Well, God be praised, he took the pledge, and the next Sunday he laid twenty-one shillings upon the chair you sit upon! Oh, didn't I give thanks upon my bended knees that night!

" 'Still I was fearful it would not last, and I spent no more than the five shillings I used to, saying to myself, May be the money will be more wanted than it is now! Well, the next week he brought me the same, and the next, and the next, until eight weeks had passed; and, glory to God, there was no change for the bad in my husband! and all the while he never asked me why there was nothing better for him out of his earnings. So I felt there was no fear for

14*

him, and the ninth week, when he came home to me, I had this table and these six chairs, one for myself, four for the children, and one for him ; and I was dressed in a new gown, and the children all had new clothes and shoes and stockings, and upon his chair I put a bran new suit, and upon his plate, I put the bill and receipt for them all, just the eight sixteen shillings, the cost that I'd saved out of his wages, not knowing what might happen, and that always went for drink. And he cried, good lady and gentleman, he cried like a baby, but 'twas with thanks to God; and now where's a healthier man than my husband in the whole county of Cork, or a happier wife than myself, or decenter or better fed children than my own ?' "

3. *Keep a good temper.*—Nothing can be more vexatious than a smoky fireside. A cold wind is sifting through the passage, and a handful of moist brushwood is sputtering under the coals, and just when you hope that it is about to kindle, a black tornado

comes whirling down the vent, and, as sooty flakes and Egyptian darkness fill the air, eyes water, nostrils tingle, the baby screams, grandmother coughs, the sash flies open, Boreas enters, and the cat disgusted leaves the room. And like that smoking chimney is the house whose presiding genius is swift to wrath, or sullen. Jaded with work, or harassed by the day's cross accidents; often drenched in the rain, or draggled by the world's rough usage, the man of toil wends homeward. "Ha, ha!" he says, "I shall soon be warm: I shall see the fire." But, alas! the fuel is green, and the chimney does not draw. Displeased by some untoward incident, or in a fretful humor, his yoke-fellow receives him with reproaches, or a frown, or treats him to long and troublous stories; and instead of the bright solace and glowing comfort, on which he vainly counted, he watches the smouldering wrath and its swelling puffs, till, in despair, he flings down the bellows, and rushes into the smokeless tempest out of doors.

No doubt a wife has many things to vex
her. Your work is hard. Your cares are
many. You have a host of things to manage; things so minute that you are not
thanked if they all go right, but at the same
time so weighty that you are exceedingly
upbraided if the least of them goes wrong.
And when your foot is on the cradle, and
the saucepan is boiling over, and the last
torn garment engages either hand, a hungry
boy or an impatient husband rushes in shout-
ing for his dinner and a dozen other things
directly. And in the midst of all that worry,
nothing is so natural as to fume and scold
and lose your temper; but in the midst of
all that worry, nothing were so noble as to
remain serene, and self-possessed, and
cheerful. And if you seek help from God,
he will enable you to possess your soul in
patience. He can give you peace and
sprightliness, and make you the ventilator
of the smoky chamber. Amid surrounding
tumult, he can supply you with soft words
and gentle looks, and, like the bird of fable,

make your very presence the antidote of storms. He can give you that cheerful countenance which doeth good like a medicine—a medicine which, if it does the patient good, does still more good to those by whom it is administered.

4. *Cultivate personal piety.*—It is a great matter for a wife and a mother to be intelligent and well-informed; for without this she can not exert a lasting ascendency over her children, nor be the fit associate of a thoughtful and strong-minded husband. But more important than a cultivated understanding is a sanctified heart. Of all possessions the most permanent, it is of all influences the most powerful; for even those who hate it most bitterly are constrained to yield it a constant though reluctant homage. Does any matter cause you grief? Like Hannah, that "woman of a sorrowful spirit," lay it before the Lord, and your countenance will be no more sad. Does any course of conduct perplex you? "In all thy ways acknowledge Him, and He will direct thy

steps." Is any undertaking completed and
can you personally do no more in order to
promote it? "Commit thy works unto the
Lord, and thy thoughts shall be established." Do you wish to be blameless in your
personal demeanor and thorough in domestic duties? Take for your guide the Word
of God; and "when thou goest it shall
lead thee; when thou sleepest it shall keep
thee; and when thou awakest it shall talk
with thee." Are you anxious to prepossess
in favor of piety the mind of your partner?
Then "be in subjection to your own husband; that if any obey not the Word, they
also may without the Word be won by the
conversation of the wives; while they behold your chaste conversation coupled with
fear (that is, your modest and respectful
demeanor). And let your adorning be, not
that outward adorning of plaiting the hair,
and of wearing of gold, or of putting on
of apparel; but let it be the ornament of a
meek and quiet spirit, which is in the sight
of God of great price."

THE UNEXPECTED GREETING.

Happy Home.

p. 167

Of all your duties the most arduous is the right training of your offspring. It is a duty which mainly devolves on you. Of all others, a mother is most constantly with her children, and of all influences her teaching, her example, and her prayers, are the likeliest to decide their future character.

Last summer a famous German writer died. His young days were the winter of his life; for, when a few weeks old he had lost his mother, and in all his rude tossings from place to place he had fallen in with no kind welcomes nor any gentle words. But somehow he contrived to get to college, and was cramming his mind with such dry learning as colleges can give, when one stormy night in the Christmas recess, he stopped at a country inn. "As I entered the parlor darkened by the evening twilight, I was suddenly wrapped in an unexpected embrace, while amid showers of tears and kisses I heard these words, 'Oh! my child —my dear child!' Though I knew that this greeting was not for me, yet the motherly pressure seemed to me the herald of better days, the beautiful welcome to a new and better world, and a sweet trembling passed over me. As soon as lighted candles came in, the illusion vanished. The modest hostess started from me in some consternation; then looking at me with smiling embarrassment, she told me that my height exactly corresponded to that of her son, whom she expected home that night from a distant school. As he did not arrive that night she tended and served me with a loving cordiality, as if to make amends to herself for the disappointment of his absence. The dainties which she had prepared for him she bestowed on me, and next morning she packed up a supply of provisions, procured me a place in the diligence, wrapped me up carefully against frost and rain, and refusing to impoverish my scanty purse by taking any payment, dismissed me with tender admonitions and motherly farewells. Yet all this kindness was bestowed, not on me, but on the image of her absent son! Such is a mother's heart! I can not describe the feelings with which I left the village. My whole being was in a strange delicious confusion." And in point of fact that motherly embrace had opened in the bosom of the orphan boy the fountain of pleasant fancies and noble feelings which have rendered Henry Zchokke the most popular story-writer, and one of the truest patriots, in all his fatherland. It was the only night when he had ever known a home, and from that brief hour he carried enongh away to give a friendly aspect to mankind, and a joyful purpose to his future life.

And, like the kind hostess, your own heart is full of motherly affection. Let it freely forth. Let your children feel how fondly you yearn toward them, and what a delight it is to you to see and make them happy. This affection is a logic which the dullest can understand, and it will insure the swiftest compliance with your wishes.

15

This cord of love is of all chains the longes*
lasting; the most vicious can not break it,
and even when you yourself are mouldering
in the clay it will moor the wayward spirit
to your memory, and keep it from much
sin. Therefore, see to it—not only that
you love them, but that you make them
conscious of your lovingness.

And then, by the attraction of your own
tenderness, seek to draw them into the love
of God. If your own be the right religion,
the living God will be your chiefest joy.
You will look up to him as your father and
friend, and will desire to move through your
dwelling and travel through the world in the
light of his constant complacency. And if
you have got this length—if through the
great Atonement you have got into the peace
of God—there will be Bible lessons in all
you do, and a living gospel in your gentle
looks. Your children will perceive that to
love God is the true way to be happy, and
whatever else it may accomplish, they will
learn to associate the religion of Jesus with

a dear parent's shining face and blame ess walk.

But, after all, if you wish to exert a hallowing influence on your children now, and if you would see them give themselves to God in the dew of their youth, you must abound in prayer as your surest and most unfailing resource. We speak of adamant and other substances as hard to fuse: we forget that the hardest of all is human will. To bring the will of your little child to the bending or melting point, needs a softening power none other than the grace of God. We speak of locks which are hard to open; we forget that the most intricate of all is the heart of man. It has wards and windings into which even a mother's love can not insinuate, and of which God's spirit only knows the way. And wherefore is it that God has given you this vehement solicitude for your children's souls, while at the same time he shows you that you can not there introduce the truths which you love, nor there enshrine the Saviour whom you yourself adore ? Wherefore, but to shut you up in lowly dependence and earnest expectancy to Him who hath the key of David, and who, when his set time comes, will open the door and take conclusive possession ? And surely, among all the supplications which reach the mercy-seat, there is none more welcome than the cry of a believing parent for her darling child. Surely, there is none which the great High Priest will present with a more gracious alacrity, or the God and Father of our Lord Jesus hear with a more divine benignity. And of all the petitions filed in the court of heaven, there is surely none less likely to be forgotten, nor one which, should you meanwhile quit this praying-ground, you may leave more confidently to the care and love of your Advocate within the vail.

But by far the happiest home is that whose heads, like Zacharias and Elisabeth, are of one mind, and who walk in the statutes and ordinances of God together. In that case, you will be able to take counsel together,

and aid one another in the anxious business
of teaching and training your children.
Your prayers on their behalf will ascend in
concert. The example of the one will not
neutralize the instructions of the other; and
whichsoever is first summoned away will
have the comfort of knowing that the work
will not stop when their teacher dies.

Having, therefore, said so much to wives
and mothers, we may perhaps be allowed,
ere closing this number, to offer a few
friendly hints to fathers and husbands. But
what better hints can we tender than the
plain directions given in the Bible long
ago?

That Bible bids married people be mu-
tually respectful. It requires the wife to
" reverence her husband," and the husband
is enjoined to " give honor to the wife."
One day, when Oberlin was eighty years
of age, in climbing a mountain he was
obliged to lean on his son-in-law, while his
wife, less infirm, walked behind by herself.
But, meeting some of his parishioners, the

good pastor felt so awkward at this apparent lack of gallantry, that he stopped to
explain the reason. Was it not a fine
feature in the old worthy's character, and
would it not be well for the world if it contained more of this Christian chivalry?
Would it not be well if it contained more
of those hallowed unions, where people
see to the last with the same admiring and
affectionate eyes with which they first
learned to love one another? And would
there not be more of these unions if people
learned to love one another "in the Lord"—
if the attachment which originated in good
sense, and congenial taste, and moral worth,
were perpetuated in Christian principle?
Piety softens the feelings and refines the
sentiments. It renders its possessor "courteous and kindly affectioned." And of
that courtesy and kind affection, who is
the rightful object, if it be not his nearest
earthly friend?

On a Saturday night you may have noticed a firm-built fellow stalking along, with

his pipe in his cheek and his hands in his
pockets, while a forlorn creature limped after
him, shifting from one tired arm to another
the laden market-basket. And in choosing
a companion for life, you were sorry that
the lazy rascal had not thought of a donkey.
But you spent the next hour with a shopmate in his own abode; and whether it
were to display the meekness of his wan
and timid consort, or to give you an august
idea of himself as a lord of creation, you
can not tell; but he always spoke to her
with such fierce contempt and vengeful bitterness, that you felt, Happy cobbler's lap-
stone! Happy torn slipper, adorning but
not confining that cobbler's fantastic toe!
Happy target on which the steam-gun flat-
tens fifty balls per minute! Happy anvil
on which Vulcan repaired old thunderbolts!
Happy all the things which people thump
and thwack and tread upon! Happier than
helpless woman with feelings thus down-
trampled! Happier than the wife whose
weary lot it is to be the anvil of an angry

temper, the target of a fiery tongue ! Yea,
happier she who, like Indian squaw, lugs
at her master's heels the heavy load, herself the truck and dray—the porter and
parcel-van !

It filled you with burning indignation ;
and we esteem you none the less for that
manly shame. It assures us that, in your
own dwelling, we shall not find you the
cold-hearted or coarse-minded despot ; and
it tells us that you are blessed with a partner whom you are proud " to have and
to hold, to love and to cherish." " Oh,
well is thee, and happy shalt thou be."
Happy are you to retain the refinement and
elevation of character, and the youthful-
ness of affection, which make the husband
still the lover ; and happy are you to have
a wife so true, and wise, and self-denied,
that to care for her comfort and share her
society are still as delightful as when first
she gave you her troth.

And yet, dear sirs, how hard it is to reach
the Bible standard of conjugal devoted-

ness! So lofty is that standard, that it
seems fitter for a pulpit text than for quota-
tion in this familiar paper. "Husbands, love
your wives, even as Christ loved the church,
and gave himself for it, that he might sanctify it, and present it to himself a glorious
church, not having spot or wrinkle, or any
such thing; but that it should be holy and
without blemish." Think of this. The
Saviour loved the church in order to make
it holy. His love was not only self-sacri-
ficing, but it was hallowing. Its tendency
and effect were to make its objects better.
And those who are joined in your sacred
relation are to take this divine example as
the model of their love. You must seek
the improvement of one another. The
consciousness of sins and defects in his disciples did not cool toward them the Saviour's
affection. It only excited his tender sagacity and faithful skill to attempt their remo-
val; and by gracious methods, one by one,
he cured their infirmities. There was no
arrogance in his tone, no disdain in his

spirit; no haste nor vexation in his manner; but so mollifying was his gentleness,
and so mild was his sanctity, that when he
healed the fault he did not hurt the feelings.
And had we something of his high purpose,
there would be little danger of affection decaying. There would be no risk of fault-
finding, and no temptation to connive at
sin. Reproofs would not break the head;
and there would be no longer need that love
should be blind.

And let us hope that you will contribute
a father's authority to a mother's tenderness
in the effort to bring up a devout and pious
family. We trust that there is no need to
inscribe the deprecating sentence on your
door.* We trust that yours is a family
which calls upon God's name. Teach
your children to be loving and generous to
one another, and promptly obedient to their

* Alluding to the words chalked on the doors of infected houses during the plague of London, Philip Henry used to say, "If the worship of God be not in the
house, write, 'Lord, have mercy upon us!' on the
door."

mother and you. Seek to fill their minds
with veneration of God, and with early ab-
horrence of sin. See to it that your own
conduct be obviously ruled by Bible maxims,
and let your appeal be direct and frequent
" to the law and to the testimony." Sustain
no frivolous excuse for absence at the hour
of prayer and try by all means to endear
the sanctuary. Like the good citizen, sung
by transatlantic bard :*—

> " His hair is crisp, and black, and long,
> His face is like the tan;
> His brow is wet with honest sweat,
> He earns whate'er he can,
> And looks the whole world in the face,
> For he owes not any man.

> " He goes on Sunday to the church,
> And sits among his boys ;
> He hears the parson pray and preach ;
> He hears his daughter's voice
> Singing in the village choir,
> And it makes his heart rejoice."

Which leads us to notice, lastly, that
nothing makes the fireside so cheerful as a

* Longfellow's " Village Blacksmith."

blessed hope beyond it. Even when you
sit most lovingly there — though the daily
task is completely done, and the infant in
the cradle is fast asleep — though this is
Saturday night, and to-morrow is the day
of rest — though the embers are bright, and
from its fat and poppling fountain in yon
coal the jet of gas flames up like a silver
cimiter; and though within your little
chamber all is peace, and warmth, and snug
repose — the roaring gusts and rattling drops
remind you that it still is winter in the world.
And when that withered leaf tapped and
fluttered on the window, mother, why was
it that your cheek grew pale, and something glistened in your eye? You thought
it perhaps might come from the churchyard
sycamore, and it sounded like a messenger
from little Helen's grave. It said, "Father
and mother, think of me." Yes, dreary
were the homes of earth were it not for the
home in Heaven. But see to it that yourselves be the Saviour's followers, and then
to you he says, " Let not your heart be

troubled ! In my Father's house are many mansions : I go to prepare a place for you." And when you come to love that Saviour rightly, you will love one another better, more truly, and more tenderly. And, trusting to meet again in that world where they neither marry nor are given in marriage, a purifying hope and a lofty affection will hallow your union on earth. And, if not inscribed above your mantel-shelf, there will at least be written in your deepest self the motto, sent to his bride by that illustrious scholar, Bengel :—

> " Jesus in heaven ;
> Jesus in the heart ;
> Heaven in the heart;
> The heart in heaven "

16

DAY-DREAMS.

CASPAR RAUCHBILDER was a German, abstruse of mind, and able of body. From his ancestors he inherited a blond complexion and a talent for boiling sugar, so that he had no trouble in acquiring either. His calling he pursued far eastward of London's famous tower, somewhere near the docks, and where many chimneys feed the murky air of Wapping. But the thick atmosphere suited Caspar's thoughtful turn ; it favored mental abstraction, and kept aloof those obtrusive materialisms which he deemed the main obstacles to transcendental discovery. His favorite motto was, " *Ex fumo dare lucem;*"* and, in order to enhance the partial opacity of his abode, he plied a perpetual meerschaum. He used to say that it was no wonder that the Egyp-

* "Smoke is the sire of light ;"—a witty allusion to the lampblack in printers' ink.

CASPAR RAUCHBILDER.

Happy Home. p. 182

tians were the wisest nation of antiquity,
after three days of such glorious darkness
as they had once enjoyed; and he often
thought that if, like a celebrated lawyer, he
could live in a cavern, he would yet be
able to throw some light on the world.

It was the ninth of November, and Caspar's more frivolous companions had gone
to the lord-mayor's show. They went,
but they saw it not. Like the railway
train, which dives from rustic gaze into the
heart of a mountain, the show was tunnel-
ing its invisible progress through the heart
of a London fog, and it was only by the
snort of trombones and the racket of drums
that cockaigne was conscious when civic
majesty passed along. Our sage found
higher employment for the holyday. Just
as the candle in a sixpenny cathedral —
such as Italian stucco merchants display
on area-rails — just as that candle begins to
come red and green through the colored
windows, when evening shrouds the city,
and street-lamps are being lit, so Caspar

was conscious this misty day of bright gleams in his censorium; and he determined on improving the inward light. Before the fire he hung a shaggy coat, which he called a bosom friend; and it deserved the name. The bosom friend was somewhat damp, for the fog had beaded all the nap with a dirty dew. And on the table Caspar placed a German sausage and a dish of Hamburg kraut. But, ere clogging his faculties with this slight refection, our philosopher thought good to improve the fit of inward clear-seeing with which he then and there felt visited. Accordingly, settling down in his easy chair, and inspissating the atmosphere with volumes of tobacco, he began to see his way through the system of the universe.

And it was not long before the sugar-boiler beheld himself a social reformer. He recollected how often he had seen the gray or yellow dust arrive at their factory, and leave it the brilliant sugar-loaf. And in that raw article he viewed an emblem of human nature, as it comes from the hand of priests and princes, and in that sugar-loaf he saw human nature as it quits the mill of the philosopher. There is first the boiling *in vacuo.* He would put society into the caldron, but would be careful not to raise the temperature above hot water. And, in order to secure a perfect vacuum, he would relieve it of all prejudices and all property. He would pump off those national codes and positive faiths which now weigh with tremendous pressure on the human soul; and as soon as that was accomplished, it would be the work of a moment to bring sentiment and principle into a state of absolute solution — the first object to be sought by a regenerator of the social system. The next business is to clarify the melted mass. Nothing can be easier. "In our works," pursued the seer, "have we not a filter of charred bones? and have I not seen the current pass into that strainer brown as sherry, and quit it clear as crystal? In like manner

16*

let us burn the bones of the old beliefs and
the outworn decencies. Ha, ha! they are
now but skeletons! And from the ashes
we will make a filter, through which this
selfish age shall pass and emerge a new
moral world. And then, in order to preserve this sweet sirup of refined humanity,
it must be caught in moulds, and consoli-
dated, and cast, and kept. For this pur
pose, one recommends as the best form
pyramids, and Fourier doats about phalanxes. But these simpletons had never
seen a sugar factory. Their purblind optics
were never blessed with the sight of an
unbroken sugar-loaf. Talk of circles, phalanxes, and pyramids, as if nature abhorred
the cone! Is it not the most comprehensive
of all figures, embodying the triangle, the
circle, the ellipse, the parabola, the hyper-
bola? and the most graceful, suggesting at
once the solidity of the pyramid, and the
curving fullness of the sphere? Away with
all compromise! I vow to reconstruct
society on the only perfect model. I shall

teach every man to be the lover of all, and
the friend of none; and this pure and
public-spirited product I shall fix — I shall
stereotype. While yet fluent and limpid,
I shall draw it off into moulds ready-made;
and in cones of concord, in sugar-loaves
of sympathy, society will crystallize into
its final and perfect organization. And
should there settle down at the inverted
apex any dregs of the old system, is there
not the turning-lathe to pare away the anti-
social feculence? All shall be alike tal
ented, alike strong and healthy; and all
equally amiable, rich, and happy. Our
crest must be the sugar-cone; our motto,
SOLIDITY, SINCERITY, SUAVITY."

At this point of the speculation, there
mingled with the odor of meerschaum a
smell more akin to burning bones. It was
not an old belief or an outworn morality,
but the peajacket too near the fire. The
bosom friend was burning. Caspar brushed
the singed and smoking nap, and put his
fingers through the brown and crumbling

skirt; and, lighting a lamp, he found that a neighboring cur had played an old prank, and stolen the sausage during his revery. However, Caspar comforted himself. The cur had stolen the sausage, but he had left the sauer-kraut and the sugar-loaf theory.

Should the reader be acquainted with any of the works lately published on the organization of labor and the reconstruction of society, he will not laugh at the reveries of Caspar Rauchbilder. Nor will he expect us to refute them. If it be idle work to build castles in the air, it is idle work besieging them.

We know, however, that such speculations are interesting to two classes of readers. There are some profligate persons who catch at everything which puts good for evil, or which offers to relieve them from moral obligation. They are tired of their wives and children; they are tired of working; they are tired of honesty; they would fain be fingering the hard-earned savings of their fellow-laborers; and they do not like

the Christian ordinance, "If any man will
not work, neither shall he eat." They
would be glad to have the pocket of the
shadowless man, so that if hungry they might
produce a tray with green pease and smoking
cutlets, or if drowsy they might put in their
hand and pull out a posted bed with its
blankets. But as the shadowless man will
not part with his pocket, they will be content, as next best, to eat their neighbor's
cutlet and sleep in their neighbor's blankets.

But besides the lazy and licentious, to
whom all such schemes are welcome, we
believe that at this moment many an industrious man feels so unhappy, that he would
hail any change in the social system as a
possible change for the better. And if, like
us, he has read some of the glowing invec-
tives and prophecies of these eager specu-
lators, the wish may very naturally prove
father to the thought, and he may fancy that
nothing except a rearrangement of society
is needful to bring about a golden age.

We, too, are social reformers. We see

many things which grieve us. We see
much extravagance among the rich, and
much improvidence among the poor. We
see a great deal of pride and bitterness.
We see the pride of rank, which believes
that itself is porcelain and that common men
are clay. We see the bitterness of penury,
which resents the wealth of others as a crime,
and which deems it a proof of spirit to in-
sult a man of higher station. We see a
fearful amount of tyranny. We see the
tyranny of squires and capitalists, refusing
to their tenants and their servants the enjoyment of the sabbath and freedom to worship God. And we see the tyranny of
working-men, compelling their fellows to
connive at crime, and enforcing compliance
with unreasonable rules, often by means of
the greatest cruelty. These things we know,
and we mourn over them. We long to see
them all redressed. We long to see the
rich less stiff, and reserved, and haughty.
We long to secure for cottages and cabins,
not only the Christmas dole, but the kind

words, and the friendly recognition, and the occasional call. We long to see toleration and fair play. We long to see industry and a competency convertible terms ; and we long to see the laborious classes kindly affectioned one to another, and respectful of the rights and the feelings of their hardworking brethren. And on every side we long to see more magnanimity, more confidence, and more mutual forbearance.

But we have no faith in any social reform which overlooks the fact that man is a fallen being. Though we had never read it in the Bible, we think we could read it in the world, that man is no longer what a holy Creator made him. *His heart is not right with God, nor is it right with his fellows.* And every ameliorating scheme which overlooks this twofold depravity is sure to end in frustration.

For many ages the mechanical world labored to create a perpetual motion. As soon as a man had learned a little algebra, or a little of the art of engine-making, he

attacked this doughty problem.   And you
may have seen some of the quaint contrivances which resulted from these attempts;
cylinders revolving to ever-falling weights
within them, and polished balls descending
a self-restoring incline.   But as discovery
advanced, it was found that all these efforts
were based on a false assumption: that they
forgot the force called FRICTION.   And as
it is now generally conceded that the dis-
coverer of this sleepless mechanism will be
the first man who annihilates the attraction
of matter, perpetual motion is reserved for
the amusement of those eccentric geniuses
who are best kept from mischief by a perpetual puzzle, and is seldom studied except
in such colleges as Hanwell and St. Luke's.

But the problem which has been abandoned in physics is now revived in the domain of ethics, and people ask, " How are
we to create within the race a constant
progress toward perfection ?   Taking man
as he is, and taking such aids as he can
nimself supply, how are we to abolish mis-

ery, and make the earth a second paradise?"
And many solutions have been offered.
The press teems with them. One day last
summer we read the plan most popular.
The brilliant writer proposes that the working men of France should resolve themselves, or that government should group
them, into huge industrial families, for five
francs apiece working eight hours a day;
leaving it to each man's sense of honor how
busily he shall labor, and requiring the
clever and the diligent to support the stupid
and the lazy. And when we read it, we
said to ourselves, "perpetual motion once
more! This sanguine projector has overlooked friction. The scheme might answer
with angelic operatives; but if tried in a
world like ours, there are two things which
will bring it to a speedy stand-still : the one
is man's irreligion ; the other is his selfishness. He would need to be a true philanthropist who would work with a steady eye
to his neighbor's welfare; and he would
need to be a God-fearing man who would

17

persist to labor when he knew that, if he slept or played, his neighbors would labor for him." And, curiously enough, the same day brought an American paper of May 13, where, among other news, we read, "While socialism is going up in Europe, it is going down in this country. The Northampton association of industry was abandoned, after having incurred a debt of 40,000 dollars, and Hopedale has relinquished the community principle, and goes upon the individual plan." And so must it ever be, till the two grand obstacles are done away. Till irreligion is exchanged for piety, and till selfishness is superseded by brotherly love, the world must proceed on the individual plan. And till then, Hopedale must count on many disappointments, and old Discord will resume his reign in the halls of each New Harmony.

Some people once built a bridge; but it was scarcely erected when it tumbled down. They tried it a second time with no better success. And a third time they changed

the plan, and took every precaution, and
allowed a long interval for the mortar to
harden ; but no sooner had they removed
the centrings than up sprang the key-stone,
and in bulged the arches, and with a crash
and a plunge the wholesale ruin poured
into the tide below.   On this, a council of
practical men was convened.   The architect came, armed with his plans so prettily
drawn, which he flourished as on a field-
day a marshal will flourish his baton.   And
rival architects came, not so much to suggest, as to enjoy a little quiet exultation.
But the man of skill, and the main hope of
the conclave, was a civil engineer from the
capital.   For a long time he said nothing ;
but he had evidently scanned it all in a single glance, and it was clear that he was only tracing symbols in the dust with his cane,
till the common herd had talked themselves
out, and he should be summoned to pronounce his oracle.   " Of course," was that
oracle, " the span is too wide, and the
ellipsis by far too eccentric."—" Impossi-

ble !" said the horrified architect ; " the first
plan had arches as round as the Roman,
and it went like a house of cards." This
by no means shook the judgment of the
man of skill ; but it emboldened a plain
man, who once wrought as a mason in that
country-side, but who had saved a little
money, and was now doing business on his
own behalf. " Truly, sirs, I wonder that
you think of nothing but arches, and abut-
ments, and spans. Just look at that brick ;"
and so saying, in his great hand he crushed
a fragment as if it were touchwood or toad-
stool. " I never knew a brick come from
these fields which would bear the weight
of its neighbor. It is not the fault of the
plan ; it is all the blame of the bricks."
And it would be well if projectors in politics
and morals adverted more to THE STRENGTH
OF THEIR MATERIALS. Like bricks from
the same kiln, some specimens of human
nature may be better than others ; but in
building a social structure for Britain or the
world, you must look, not to picked sam-

ples, but to the ordinary run. You must look not to patriots, and saints, and the martyrs of favorite schemes; but you must look at your neighbors, and your shopmates, and the mass of your fellow-townsmen, and say if you are prepared to cast away all your present securities for peace and comfort, and fling yourself entirely on the honor of each and the charities of all? For if you distrust your neighbors as they are, no new arrangement into groups or ateliers, into phalanxes or cones, will make them trustworthy. A few bad bricks will spoil the finest arch; but the finest arch will not convert to marble or adamant blocks of untempered clay.

We love our fellow-men, and we long for their greater happiness; but so profoundly do we believe that "the imagination of man's heart is only evil"—so persuaded are we that our world, as yet, contains little loyalty to God, and little love of man to man—that we have no faith in any self-restoring system. It is not a new construc-

17*

tion which society needs, so much as new material. Nor can we promise ourselves a political millennium. Doubtless it is the duty of every citizen to give efficiency to such good government as he enjoys; and it is the duty of every state to aim at constitutional optimism; to seek such a code of laws, and such a distribution of power, as will make it easiest for the citizens to do what is right, and most difficult to do what is wrong. But there is no magic in political change. No form of government— republican, representative, or despotic— can cure the real complaint of our species. No law can change vice into virtue, or give to guilt the joys of innocence. No ruler can make the atheist happy, or kindle a blessed hope in that mephitic mind which has quenched its own lamp of immortality. When Hercules put on the poisoned robe, it did not matter where he went: no change of climate, no breezy height, no balmy sky could lull the venom in his fiery veins. Restless and roaming, he wandered to and fro, and raged at everything; but the real quarrel was with his tainted self, and the change which would have relieved his misery would have been a migration from his own writhing nerves and stounding bones. And let a man of idle or immoral habits, or let an ill-assorted family, try all the constitutions in the world — or let a new constitution come to their own country once a-year — and they will soon discover that to a guilty conscience, or a dissolute character, political day-springs bring no healing. Legislation contains no charm — no spell for converting personal or domestic wretchedness into virtue and tranquillity; and so long as a man is entangled in his own corruption — so long as he wears the poisoned vest of inherent depravity — "he may change the place, but he can not cheat the pain."

Is there, then, you will ask, no hope for society? Is the present routine of selfishness, oppression, and suffering, to go on for ever? Assuredly not. But it will

come to an end in no other way except
that which God has designed and foretold.
It will end when he himself interposes.
Till then, visionaries, amiable or atheistic,
may each propound his panacea; but, alas!
the plague of society is too virulent for any
medicine native to our earth. And no
doubt elaborate attempts will be made, and
associations will be formed, with a view to
counteract the dispersive elements in human nature. Influential leaders, poetical
statesmen, and discarded projectors, will
say, "Go to, let us build us a city and a
tower, whose top may reach unto heaven,
and let us make us a name, lest we be scattered abroad upon the face of the whole
earth;" but the feuds and the jargon which
confounded the plain of Shinar, will prove
fatal to Babel the Second. And it is not
till the Prince of Peace shall commence
his reign of righteousness, and, simulta-
neous with his enthronement, the Spirit of
God shall mollify the minds of men, that
' violence" shall vanish from our earth,

and " wasting and destruction" from within
its borders. And when that day comes —
when, by the direct interference of the
Holy Spirit, man's enmity to God is con-
verted into allegiance and love, and man's
selfishness is drowned in kindness and good-
will — many of the results for which men at
present sigh will no longer need perilous
experiments, but will develop of their own
accord. When the years are all one pen-
tecost, and the world one Christian family,
none will lack, and, if they please, people
may then have " all things in common."*
" For as the earth bringeth forth her bud,
and as the garden causeth the things that
are sown in it to spring forth ; so the Lord
God will cause righteousness and praise to
spring forth before all the nations."

And, in the meanwhile, the reader may
secure his own happiness without overturn-
ing an empire or new-moulding society.
Like Caspar Rauchbilder, you run the risk
of losing some solid and immediate advan-

* Acts ii. and iv.

tages, while musing on remote and wholesale reformations. The present state of
society may be vicious; but, in the most
essential matters, your Creator has rendered
you independent of society. By making
you the custodier of your own soul, he has
made you the keeper of your own comfort.
And if you be wise, you will go so far on
the individual plan as to study the gospel,
and seek the one thing needful for yourself.
So far as you are concerned, that gospel is
a personal message. To you and me, my
brother, God offers a personal salvation.
And if we believe that gospel, and live
godly, righteous, and sober in the world,
whatever be the state of society, we shall
secure our personal happiness here and
hereafter. Perhaps, too, we shall then be
able to do something in order to mitigate
the misery and increase the happiness of
those around us.

FIRE-FLIES.

In the New World's warmer forests they find great numbers of a shining fly ;* and so plentiful is their light that people often turn them to useful purposes. A friend of our own, when his ship lay anchored off the coast, had occasion to search for a book in the cabin overnight, and recollecting that two of these living lanterns were enclosed in a pill-box, with their aid he ran over the titles of the different volumes, till he found the one he wanted. The natives often keep a few in a vial, to guide them at little turns of household work; and as there is no dan ger of their causing combustion, travellers sometimes put one of these vials along with their watch, and under their pillow.

Of such tiny lights we now send the reader a specimen. It is not the object of

* Elater noctilucus, a sort of beetle.

these tracts to give a system of theology, but we should be glad if we could impart the A B C of Christianity; and in studying its early lessons, our fire-flies may lend a little light. Thankful should we be if they proved of service to any one journeying in the dark, and perplexed about his road; or if they shed a ray, however feeble, on any sentence of God's own word. And though grown people may despise them, we are not without the hope that, like the flying lamps in Chili, they may find favor with your boys and girls.

THE PILGRIMS AND THEIR PITCHERS.

It was long ago, and somewhere in the eastern clime. The king came into the garden and called the children round him. He led them up to a sunny knoll and a leafy arbor on its summit. And when they had all sat down, he said, "You see far down the river, and hanging as on the side of the hill, yon palace? It is a palace—though here it looks so little and far away. But when you reach it you will find it a larger and sweeter home than this: and when you come you will find that I have got there before you. And when you arrive at the gate, that they may know that you belong to me, and may let you in, here is what each of you must take with him." And he gave to each of the children a most beautiful alabaster jar——a little pitcher so exquisitely fashioned that you were almost afraid to touch it, so pure that you could see the daylight through it, and with delicate figures raised on its sides. "Take this, and carry it carefully. Walk steadily, and the journey will soon be over." But they had not gone far before they forgot. One was running carelessly and looking over his shoulder, when his foot stumbled, and as he fell full length on the stony path the pitcher was shivered in a thousand pieces; and one way and another, long, long before they reached the palace, they had broken all the pitchers. When this

18

happened I may mention what some of them did. Some grow sulky, and knowing that it was of no use to go forward without the token, they began to shatter the fragments still smaller, and dashed the broken sherds among the stones, and stamped them with their feet; and then they said, "Why trouble ourselves about this palace? It is far away, and here is a pleasant spot. We will just stay here and play." And so they began to play. Another could not play, but sat wringing his hands, and weeping bitterly. Another grew pale at first, but recovered his composure a little on observing that his pitcher was not broken so bad as some others. There were three or four large pieces, and these he put together as well as he could. It was a broken pitcher that could hold no water, but by a little care he could keep it together; and so he gathered courage, and began to walk along more cautiously. Just then, a voice accosted the weeping boy, and looking up he saw a very lovely form, with a sweet and

THE PILGRIM AND THE PITCHERS.

Happy Home   p. 207

pleasant countenance — such a countenance as is accustomed to be happy, though something for the present has made it sad. And in his hand he held just such a pitcher as the little boy had broken, only the workmanship was more exquisite, and the colors were as bright as the rainbow round the stranger's head. "You may have it," he said; "it is better than the one you have lost, and though it is not the same, they will know it at the gate." The little mourner could scarcely believe that it was really meant for him; but the kind looks of the stranger encouraged him. He held out his hand for the stranger's vase, and gave a sob of joyful surprise when he found it his own. He began his journey again, and you would have liked to see how tenderly he carried his treasure, and how carefully he picked his steps, and how sometimes, when he gave another look at it, the tear would fill his eye, and he lifted up his happy thankful face to heaven. The stranger made the same offer to the playing boys, but by this time they were so bent on their new amusements, that they did not care for it. Some saucy children said, he might lay his present down and leave it there if he liked, and they would take it when they wanted it. He passed away, and spoke to the boy who was carrying the broken pitcher. At first he would have denied that it was broken, but the traveller's clear glance had already seen it all; and so he told him, " You had better cast it away, and have this one in its stead." The boy would have been very glad to have this new one, but to throw away the relics of his own was what he could never think of. They were his chief dependence every time he thought of the journey's end; so he thanked the stranger, and clasped his fragments firmer. The boy with the gift-pitcher and this other reached the precincts of the palace about the same time. They stood for a little and looked on. They noticed some of the bright-robed inhabitants going out and in, and every time they passed the gate, they

presented such a token as they themselves
had once got from the king, but had broken
so long ago. The boy who had accepted
the kind stranger's present now went forward, and held it up; and whether it was
the light glancing on it from the pearly gate,
I can not tell, but at that instant its owner
thought that it had never looked so fair.
He who kept the gate seemed to think the
same, for he gave a friendly smile, as much
as to say, " I know who gave you that;"
and immediately the door was lifted up and
let the little pilgrim in. The boy with the
broken pitcher now began to wish that his
choice had been the same; but there was
no help for it now. He adjusted the fragments as skilfully as he could, and trying
to look courageous, carried them in both
his hands. But he who kept the gate was
not to be deceived. He shook his head,
and there was that sorrow in his look which
leaves no hope. The bearer of the broken
pitcher still held fast his useless sherds,
and lingered long. But no one took any

18*

notice of him, or felt the smallest pity for him; and though he made many efforts, every time he approached the door it seemed of itself to shut again.*

THE ROYAL FEAST.

A CERTAIN king prepared a feast in honor of his dear and only son. And the first invitations he issued to the nobles of the land, and some ancient families who had been long in favor with the prince. But when the appointed hour arrived a sulky fit had seized them, and, as if by previous concert, scarcely one of them appeared. But

* Perhaps you will understand this story by laying the following texts together :—

" Without holiness no man shall see the Lord."—Heb. xii. 14.

" God made man upright."—Eccl. vii. 29.

" All have sinned and come short of the glory of God."—Rom. iii. 23.

" All the world is guilty before God. And by the deeds of the law there shall no flesh be justified in his sight."—Rom. iii. 19, 20.

" But now THE RIGHTEOUSNESS OF GOD is manifested; even the righteousness of God which is by faith of Jesus Christ, unto all and upon all them that believe.

resolved that his munificence should not
be lost, nor the honor intended for his son
defeated, and as all the people there around
were equally his subjects, he said to his
servants, " The feast is ready, but the guests
are not come.   Go into the streets and
hedges, and bring in whomsoever you find."
Forth went the servants, and great was the
wonder when they announced their errand.
A poor laborer was returning from his work,
and having got no wages from his master,
was trudging wearily home to his empty
cupboard, when the king's messenger hailed
him, and told him that a feast was prepared
for him.   After the first gaze of incredulity,

Being justified freely by his grace, through the redemption that is in Christ Jesus: whom God hath set forth
to be a propitiation, through faith in his blood."—Rom.
iii. 21, 22, 24, 25.

"Therefore being justified by faith, we have peace
with God through our Lord Jesus Christ: by whom
also we have access by faith into this grace wherein we
stand, and rejoice in hope of the glory of God."—Rom.
v. 1, 2.

"But they being ignorant of God's RIGHTEOUS-
NESS, and going about to establish their own righteousness, have not submitted themselves unto the righteousness of God."—Rom. x. 3.

finding that he carried this commission from his king, and was really in earnest, the poor laborer turned his steps toward the palace. The next was a cripple, who sat by the wayside, begging. He had gathered little that day, when the messenger told him he would find a feast at the palace, and the king desired to see him. The lame man had heard that something remarkable was going on at the court, and that the king was giving an entertainment in honor of some special event in his son's history; and though he expected no more than a loaf of bread and a flagon of wine at the gate, as he knew that the king was of a very sumptuous and gracious disposition, he did not hesitate, but raised himself on his crutches, got up, and hobbled away. Then the messenger came to a shady lane, down which a retired old gentleman lived on a small spot of ground of his own. The messenger had far more trouble with him. It was not so much that he questioned the message, or that he did not like the invita

tion, but that he was annoyed at its abrupt-
ness and his own want of preparedness.
He asked if there were to be no more invitations issued next week, or if there were
no possibility of postponing the visit till the
following evening ; for, considering his station in society, he would like to appear in
his best, and could have been glad of a little leisure to get all things in order. "However," said the messenger, "you know the
custom of our court—the king provides
the robes of state—all things are ready,
come away ;" and as he posted on, the old
householder thought that rather than run
any risk, he had better go at once—though
some noticed that as he passed along he
occasionally eyed his thread-bare garment
with a look that seemed to say, he could
have put on better, had longer time been
allowed him. Then at the palace it was
interesting to see how the different parties
acted. According to the custom o˙ that
country, and more especially after the mag-
nificent manner of that king, each guest was

furnished on his arrival with a gorgeous
robe. They were all alike, exceeding rich
and costly ; and, the moment he came up,
one was handed to each new-comer, and he
put it on, and passed in to the dazzling
banquet-hall. Some awkward persons, who
did not know the usage of the place, and
who had carried with them the mean notions which they learned among the high-
ways and hedges, scrupled to receive these
shining robes, and asked what price they
must pay for them. And one individual was
observed to come in with rather better attire
than the rest, and when offered a robe of
the king's providing, he politely declined
it, and stepped forward into the state-apart-
ments. He was no sooner there than he
rued his vanity — for his faded tinsel con-
trasted fearfully with the clothing of wrought
gold in which the other guests were arrayed.
However, instead of going back to get it
changed, he awaited the issue. All things
were ready ; the folding-doors opened, and
from chambers all-radiant with purest light,

and redolent of sweetest odors, amidst a joyful train the king stepped in to see the company. A frown for a moment darkened his majestic brow as he espied the presumptuous guest, but the intruder that instant vanished ; and, with a benignity which created in every soul such a joy as it had never felt before — with a look which conferred nobility wherever it alighted, and a smile that awakened immortality in every bosom — he bade them welcome to the ivory palace, and told them to forget their father's house and their poor original, for he meant to make them princes every one, and as there were many mansions in the house they should there abide for ever.*

THE BLASTED BOWER.

Thousands of years ago, there lived a prince-philosopher. In his youth he was

---

* See Matt. xxii. 1–14; and Luke xiv. 15–24, and compare them with Isaiah xxv. 6, lv. 1–3; Phil. iii. 8, 9 ; Rev. iii. 17, 18.

single-hearted and devout. He loved to
pray, and the beautiful hymns which his
father had written he delighted to sing, and
he made some of his own as beautiful.
And the Most High God loved this pious
prince, and prospered him wonderfully.
And as, harp in hand, he sat on one of the
knolls of Zion singing Jehovah's praise,
there began to sprout and bourgeon from
the soil sweet scents and brilliant blossoms;
and as the psalm proceeded, the vines and
creepers mounted, and the tendrils took
hold of one another, till they mantled overhead, and the minstrel sang in a nest of
flowers. The young prince was very fond
of this alcove, and spent in it many a sultry
noon. But, by-and-by, he began to love
God less, and soon forgot him altogether.
He did not care to sing psalms and pray;
and a bad wife taught him to worship her
god. It was a gilded idol, shaped like a
beautiful woman; and this silly man said
his prayers to this image of gold. And at
last he took the image into his beautiful

bower : but no sooner had it entered than
a shudder passed through the alcove,
and every leaflet trembled. The jasmine
breathed sickly, the rose flung down its
petals, and the heart's-ease died. The
prince was much mortified. He vowed
that he would make the bower blossom
again. So he took a costly urn, and filled
it with a rare elixir—an infusion into
which he had melted music, and precious
gems, and daintiest delights—and poured
the voluptuous draught around the roots.
But without effect : all continued bare and
blighted. Then he filled the urn with
conquest, and with the blood-red irrigation
soaked the reeking soil. In vain. And,
last of all, he travelled far, and climbed a
lofty steep in quest of a famous dew. And
in his pilgrimage to the world-top mountain, he amassed such knowledge as no mortal had ever gleaned before. He learned
the entire of things, and spake of birds and
beasts and fishes ; and when he returned
so wondrous wise, his compatriots raised a

shout with which the welkin vibrates still.
And from the chalice he poured the hoard-
ed draught—the largest flood of fame ever
wasted on weary land.   But still there was
nothing seen except the wiry trellis against
the burning sky; and on his blasted bower
the broken-hearted monarch wrote, "Vanity of vanities, all is vanity."

Years passed on, and, visiting the spot,
the soul of the prince was moved.   It felt
as if all his youth had been a balmy trance
in this bower of blessedness, and as if he
had tasted no real joy since then.   And,
observing beneath the withered canopy the
crumbling stock of Ashtaroth, he seized
the rotten pagod and hurled it far away.
Then, sinking on the ground in a paroxysm
of bitter grief, he cried, " My Father, my
God, wert not thou the guide of my youth?"
His spirit relented.   To the God of his
early adoration he felt his early love returning, and soon sank into a sleep which in-
genuous shame and godly sorrow pervaded
As he woke, the smell of a delicious flower

startled a youthful memory; and, gazing upward, roses of Sharon looked down through the lattice, while among them, like pulses of Paradise, exquisite odors went and came. Heaven's window had opened while the penitent slept, and had sent a plenteous rain. And rising from the fragrant couch, as a conclusion of the whole matter, and as the business of his remaining days, Solomon wrote this inscription: "Fear God, and keep his commandments: for this is the whole duty of man."*

THE VOYAGE.

There was a man who owned a little ship, and carried on in it a petty coasting trade. He used to creep from port to port, and bought or bartered such commodities as each supplied. And being fond of knowledge and strange sights, he sometimes landed and visited the interior, and

* For the key, consult the Book of Ecclesiastes, and 1 Kings, xi.

noted down any curious thing he came upon.*

But being of a wistful and aspiring turn, he often longed to spread a bolder sail, and make some nobler land.† He had heard the rumor of brighter climes; a whisper of spicy forests and dazzling wings; a distant report of waters which mature the pearl, and rivers which run down gold.‡ But the rumor was vague, and stirred no effort; and so our merchantman still cruised about from one dingy port to another of the little island where he was born: till one day, talking to a friend, and lamenting his joyless life, his labor without profit, and his success without satisfaction, he was surprised to learn that his friend had long felt the same. Nay, more: he had been making inquiry, and had resolved on forsaking his present line of life. He had learned that the Lord of that better land was a most kind and generous Prince, and made all strangers welcome, provided that,

* Eccl. i. 16, 17.   † Psalms, lv. 6.   ‡ 1 Cor. ii. 9.

ere setting out, they secured a passport,
which was freely supplied to all who chose.
And he had gained some information regarding the country itself. The exact distance
he could not tell. Some had reached it in
a few weeks, and others had been at sea
for several years. But he had procured
a chart in which the course was clearly
marked, and the grand port of arrival set
down. And, for his own part, he was sick
of this wretched coast, which yielded nothing except the lust of the flesh, and the
lust of the eye, and the pride of life; and
he was determined to lose no time in setting sail for Immanuel's land.

Delighted with the information, and furnished with the chart, our voyager also
resolved to steer for this better country.
And, like one into whom a mighty purpose
has entered, there was great alacrity in his
movements, and much energy in his prep-
arations. He might sometimes be seen for
hours bending over the chart, and familiar-
izing himself with its landmarks. And, in

his anxiety to be well-informed on the subject, he got the narratives of some distinguished mariners who had performed the
voyage lately; but after reading several, he
found that they all agreed in extolling the
minuteness and fidelity of the chart; and
always ended by saying, that whosoever
took heed to his track, according to its
markings, could never go wrong.*

At last he set sail. It was a bright and
airy morning when his little vessel turned
her head to sea. In the healthy flutter
overhead, he heard a promise of better
things to come, and the thought, "Bound
for the better land," put springs into his
feet as he paced the exulting deck. The
very clouds, which scurried light and pure
along the sky, he hailed as friends and fel-
low-voyagers, for they, too, seemed to seek
that brighter shore; and the faith and hope
with which his whole nature swelled and
thrilled, at last melted into love and wonder; and with uplifted hands he cried,

* Psalm cxix. 9, 99.

"Blessed be the God and Father of our
Lord Jesus Christ, who, according to his
abundant mercy, hath begotten me to a
lively hope—to an inheritance incorrup-
tible and undefiled, and that fadeth not
away;" and presently, on bended knees,
he was pouring out the gratitude of his
ravished heart to the glorious Lord of that
land.

He was getting clear of the roads when
he noticed a lighthouse rising up from the
water, and looking to the chart, he found
that it was erected over the Demas sands.*
And just here a pilot-boat came alongside
of him, bearing despatches from the shore.
One was a letter reminding him of his en-
gagement to grace with his presence a
splendid rout, which was to come off next
day, and reminding him that it was partly
in honor of himself that it was given, and
they would all be so dull without him.
And the other was a letter from a near relation, telling him, that if he persisted in this

* 2 Tim. iv. 10.

ridiculous course, although he had intended to make him his heir, he would alter his will, and cut him off with a shilling. But, just at that moment, the peace of God was to keeping his mind, that neither message disturbed him. He remembered, " Be not conformed to the world: love not the world, neither the things that be of the world ;" and having written two brief but decisive notes, he turned the vessel's head a point more to seaward, and cleared in safety the Demas sands.

After this the breeze abated, and toward noon it was nearly calm. Our voyager was in high spirits at the moral victory which he had just achieved, and was now pretty sure that he had not only set out in the right direction, but that, at this rate, nothing could hinder him from landing aright. A little self-complacency sprang up in his mind, and he thought less about the kindness of Him who had invited him to the goodly realm, than about his own luck or wisdom in actually going. And while he was thus musing, he wondered, but he rather thought the ship was standing still. There could be no doubt of it. The sails were still a little set, and breaths of air were still moving about; but the ship was fast, and would not answer to the helm; and, looking over the side, he could see quite plainly the ridge of rock on which it had grounded. He was much amazed; for he had felt no shock nor jar, and had taken it as gently as if it had been a sunken cloud or a spell in the water. But there he was, fast and firm · and it was no use backing the sails, for he could not move, and, to make the matter worse, the tide was ebbing. Just then, he noticed a sail near hand, and signalled her. She proved to be his old friend, who had first suggested the idea of this voyage, and who himself had newly put to sea.

Voyager. Well, here's an ugly trap. Do you know what they call this horrid reef?

Friend. Self-confidence. There is not a worse shoal in all the passage.

V. Why, then, is there no light nor beacon over it?

F. There are these buoys. And what is the use of your sounding-line?*

V. But was it not curious that I should slide so softly on what you say is such a dangerous rock?

F. Well, it was just in the same way that the good ship Galatia was wrecked long ago. She had just parted with the best pilot who ever navigated those seas — the famous pilot, Paul; and the last glimpse he had of her she was running well. And when word was brought him that the hapless Galatia was fast aground of this treacherous reef, so strange and unaccountable did it seem, that he exclaimed, " O, foolish Galatians, who hath bewitched you?" But it is time you were thinking what to do; for, if rough weather find you here, you must go all to pieces.

V. And what shall I do?

F. Look yonder!

* Prov xviii. 12; Rom xi. 20; 2 Cor. xiii. 5.

And, as directed, the voyager looked aloft. And, though it was bright day, there shone in the clear firmament a broad and silvery star. The mariner knew that it was the Star of Bethlehem; and, as he intently eyed it, he felt his pinnace lifted off the reef, and soon the sails began to bulge, and, in gladness of release, the vessel bounded on her way.*

Humbled by this mismanagement, the voyager after this consulted his chart more carefully, and steered more exactly according to its minute directions. Sometimes he sailed in sunshine, sometimes in shade. At times, the currents were cross, or the gale was in the vessel's eye. And then, again, the wind blowing where it listeth, would lift him fast along, and as one bright billow handed him to another, a joyous ditty would carol from the deck. Occasionly, he had a convoy from another seeking the same port, and often without a consort he pursued his solitary way.

* Phil. iii. 3, iv. 13; Psalm cxxiv. 7.

At last, a storm arose. There was first a lull and a lurid calm. A dusky red, a bloody dimness curtained the horizon, and enclosed the ship within its thickening pall. There felt like sulphur in the air, and the breath grew short, and the strength gave way, as when some fearful thing is coming. And when the angry sun was set, and nothing sparkled in the blotted firmament, and deep was calling unto deep — the moaning signals, in which the spirits of desolation seem to ask, If all be ready? it flashed — again — again — again; and the welkin was fire, and the sea was foam; and, amid the splitting cracks, and the engulfing flame, and the rising hurricane, it felt as if the quivering skiff were a tiny morsel in destruction's open jaws. "O my God, my soul is cast down within me. Deep calleth unto deep, at the noise of thy waterspouts, all thy waves and thy billows are gone over me." It was the hour of darkness, and of the prince of the power of the air, and strange whispers hissed through the gloom or gurgled up from the weltering flood. One of them suggested, "Cast away the beginning of your confidence." Another murmured, "Curse God and die." One yelled, "Hell is but a fable, and heaven a poet's dream." And the ghastliest of all was a reptile croak, "There is no God." And the poor benighted soul began to wonder if it could be on the right track that all this riot of horrors went on, and feared that he must have got into some fiendish by-path, and almost wished, rather than hear those blasphemous voices, that the deep would swallow him quick. But from this belly of hell he cried again, and his brief but piercing prayer was ever the same, "Lord, save — or I perish." And, through all the turmoil and din, that cry was heard ; for what is yon pavilion of moving light — that sunny shrine which glides over the billows, and a glassy path spreads out before it? What is this presence from whose distant ray the phantoms of the pit have already retreated, and their foul accents died away ? The bright and morning star is already on board ; and to the " Peace, be still," which he spoke, the obsequious storm and the crouching waves have given instant answer. " It is I ; be not afraid ;" and, though still soaked in spray and cold with terror, the presence of his protector and deliverer restores the sinking soul. Assured that the Saviour himself has taken the helm, he drops into a tranquil slumber, and, when he awakes, his drenched garments are dry, and the monsoon is past, and those constant winds are entered, which will always blow the self-same way till he reaches the haven where he fain would be.

As he glances along on the gentle waters, he takes out his log-book, and enters a whole account of the hurricane. " They that go down to the sea in ships, that do business in the great waters ; these see the works of the Lord and his wonders in the deep. For he commandeth and raiseth the stormy wind, which lifteth up the waves

thereof. They mount up to the heavens,
they go down again to the depths ; their
soul is melted because of trouble. Then
they cry unto the Lord in their trouble, and
he bringeth them out of their distresses.
He maketh the storm a calm, so that the
waves thereof are still. Then are they glad
because they be quiet. Oh, that men would
praise the Lord for his goodness and for his
wonderful works to the children of men."
And from that time forward he marks a
happy change in the character of the voyage. There is more progress and less vi-
cissitude. He has passed under deeper
skies and got into steadier gales. And he
has fewer adventures and perils to record.
And he has a serene and prevailing hope
of arriving safe at last. By-and-by, he begins to notice fragments of sea-weed, and
crosses whole banks of them ; but though
they somewhat hinder the ship and make
its way more cumbrous, he does not grudge
them, for they tell that land is near. And
to tell it still more clearly, by-and-by new

shapes are seen—bright pinions and dart-
ing gems which have come from the hidden
shore, and are going back again.   And
there it comes itself—the shore with its
palm-trees waving and its snowy temple
gleaming ; and already he inhales the fresh
and balmy odor from distant forests and
unseen flowers—when some suspicious
sail bounds toward him, some skulking cor-
vette which prowls on its pirate outlook near
the very harbor's mouth, and for a moment
he marvels that such murderous robbers
should be suffered to cruise along the very
margin of Immanuel's Land.   But a signal
is made from shore, " Resist, and he will
flee."   And obedient to the timely signal,
the ship puts on her fighting trim ; and no
sooner is the flag of defiance shaken out,
than the dark sail veers about, and, as it
sneaks away, a shout pursues it, "O Grave !
where is thy victory ?   O Death ! where is
thy sting ?"   When the morrow dawned,
it showed the anchor dropped and the canvass furled ; but it was the fair haven of Im-

mortality, and the voyager had got safe to land.

___

THE DILIGENCE.

A friend of ours received an invitation to visit an illustrious prince in a foreign country. Our friend was considered a sincere and worthy man, but he had a sour and splenetic temper. In the stage which conveyed him, there were some other pas-sengers; but as they were strangers, he did not speak to them. One had a coat of a peculiar fashion, and he set him down for a fop. Another had a slight blemish on a face otherwise pleasing; but every time that our traveller turned that way, his eye was arrested by that scar. A third had a slight impediment in his speech; but though this, like the rest, was a little thing, our tourist held that nothing is a trifle in so serious a matter as looks and language. The strangers, however, seemed to be well acquainted with one another, and from some

20*

casual expressions it appeared that they
were all journeying to the same place.
They failed to make any impression on
their taciturn comrade; and, admonished
by his short answers, they were polite
enough to let him alone. It began to rain;
and as the large drops swept in on the pas-
senger opposite, he wished to put up the
glass: but his gruff neighbor demurred;
and, rather than have any debate, the gentleman wrapped himself up in his cloak,
and retiring into the corner, shunned the
shower as well as he could. And so, stage
after stage, they journeyed — the three
happy and at home with one another, the
silent man moody and self-absorbed. At
last the hills around the mansion came in
sight; and then the enclosing wall; and
then the swelling lawn, studded with its
noble trees; and last of all, the towers and
battlements of the castle itself began to
appear.

And now the passengers began to look
sprightlier, and glanced out at the win-

dows, as if they knew it all, and smiled to one another, and began to get things in readiness, as if they, too, meant to stop somewhere hereabouts. And so they did; for the moment the stage drew up at the castle-gate, they all got out, and it was evident, from the attendants in waiting, that they were distinguished visiters. Two of them were special friends of the prince, and the one who had borne the pelting of the shower so patiently was his brother. Our sullen traveller felt exceedingly awkward, and almost wished to retain his place in the vehicle and pass on. But ascertaining who he was, and that he too was bound for their mansion, the prince's brother introduced himself, and exerted all his courtesy to supersede his apologies and restore his self-possession. By the time they reached the entrance-door, the poor man's confusion had somewhat subsided; but bitter were his self-reproaches, and vehement his protestations that, if he had another journey to perform, he would not

be so haughty by the way, nor look so silly
at the journey's end.

MORAL.

Be not sectaries—be not recluses. Please
every one his neighbor for his good. Put
up the window when it rains on your fel-
low-passenger; and to do good and com-
municate, do not forget. Fall not out with
your Christian brethren by the way; and,
in order to avoid painful discoveries and
explanations when this conveyance of the
visible church stands still and the journey
of life is over, put on no arrogant nor
exclusive airs while you still are fellow-
travellers.

THE FAITHFUL SERVANT.

DEAR READER: You are away from home. Perhaps it is not long since you left it, and still your fondest thoughts are there. When the house is quiet; when you can follow every footfall in the street, till it dies away round the corner; when the fire burns low, and every tick of the clock comes loud and earnest; or when you chance to awaken up in the lonely night, your mind is sure to wander off to that loved dwelling. Where is it? Is it yon white house, with the mountain behind it, and the misty crags where the eagle screams, and the torrent thunders down, in the most ancient melody of old and tuneful Wales? Or is it far, far away, in the highlands? Is it thatched with broom and brackens, and does a peat-stack stand at the gable? and out among the crows and the peeweets, does Donald wrap round him his plaid, and herd the dun cattle, till the corn is cut and the potato-shaws are withered? Or is it an English cottage? With its little lozenge-panes does the casement unclose on hinges? and, when opened, does a sweet air come in from roses, and honeysuckle, and mignionette? Is it on the edge of the common, where sober geese and gentle donkeys browse together? and near the shaded pond, where the wagoner stops his team, and cools their fetlocks in the dusty summer? Or is it down the bushy lane, where, in harvest, blackberries and filberts ripen, and long threads of gossamer saunter about in the golden air? Or near the village church? so near, that when you lay in bed with the fever, you could hear the choir and the organ? Are there almshouses all in a row — six for old men, and six for old women? And when they marched to church on sabbath mornings, how many did you count the girls in blue frocks and white mittens? how many the boys in

THE SORROWFUL PARTING.

Happy Home.

p. 239

round caps tufted with orange tops? Oh,
yes! it was a sweet place, where you were
born and bred; and if your father and
mother are still alive, I do not wonder that
your heart is often there.

Besides, you say that you are not happy
here. The house is grand, but it is strange.
Nobody cares for you. No one cheers you
with a kind look or a pleasant word; and
if your loneliness should ever make you
dull, your fellow-servant jeers you. And
when you think of that sorrowful afternoon
when you packed up your things, and your
brother carried your box, and your father
convoyed you as far as the milestone; and
when you feel again the clasp of that dear
old hand, and seem to hear the faltering
voice, " God Almighty bless you!" your
heart is like to break, and you almost wish
that there were no servants and no mistresses, and no need for poor girls leaving home
to seek a place with strangers.

But dry that tear. I feel for you, so
young and solitary, and I would fain say

something which might comfort you. Read this letter carefully, and read it to the end.

Eighteen hundred years ago, the Son of God came down from heaven, and visited our world; and that visit of his is by far the most important event in our world's surprising story. With all the love of God, he came in all the gentleness and tenderness of man; and his errand was as kind as his nature. He came to save sinners. To purchase their pardon, he shed his blood on the cross of Calvary; and he is now gone back to heaven, a Prince and a Saviour, delighting to bestow repentance and the remission of sins. And he sends through the world his Bible and his ministers, beseeching men to take the benefit of his most precious blood, and through these ministers, and that Bible, saying, " Come unto me, all ye that labor, and are heavy laden, and I will give you rest."*

Jesus went back to heaven; but he left

* All this is explained more fully in the first three numbers of " The Happy Home."

behind him his apostles. These good men went everywhere preaching the gospel; and, as the Holy Spirit was with them, it was wonderful with what speed they came When they told the love of God in sending his dear Son, and the Saviour's love in dying, something fixed the people's ear, and the story moved their minds — fierce spirits melted, and flinty hearts flowed down; and from among the roughest of mankind the Redeemer drew disciples after him. And whether it was the soldier's barrack, or the noble's country-seat — whether it was the city-mansion, or the tanner's hut beside the shore — wherever the gospel entered, it brought holiness, and peace, and joy. But there was no class of persons to whom it was more welcome than to the servants of that time. Many of them were actual slaves. They had been torn away from their homes in the German forest or on the hills of Britain, and were now in bondage to the haughty Roman. And those of them who worked for wages were often harshly treated and poorly paid. But God is no respector of persons, and the gospel was as free to Onesimus as to his rich master, Philemon, and brought the same blessings to Rhoda, the housemaid, as to Mary, her mistress. The kindness of that gospel won the heart of many a servant. They threw away their idols—they gave up their sinful habits, and became the affectionate fol lowers of that exalted Saviour who was once himself " in the form of a servant." And as great numbers were admitted to the early church, they became a special charge to the church's ministers. Timothy and Titus preached so plainly, that the servants understood them; and when Paul and Peter wrote letters to their flocks, they usually put in a message to the servants. Their labor was not lost. Many of these converts became bright Christians. By their modesty, and diligence, and faithfulness, they commended the cause of Christ; and when times of persecution came, rather than deny their Lord they were ready to go to

prison and to death, and in the early an-
nals of your class have left their martyr
names.

The Lord Jesus is gone back to heaven;
but he desires that you too would become
his disciple. He desires that you would
come to him to receive pardon for your
sins, and to get a new and right nature.
He desires that you would enter his household and become his servant for ever. And
he offers to become to you the same gracious Saviour and the same Almighty Friend
as he has been to the thousands of happy
servants before you.

Believe the blessed Saviour, and your
worst sorrows will be ended. Your earthly lot may be hard. Your work may be
irksome, your wages small, your employer
severe. Never mind; you have promotion
in prospect. The poor people who come
begging to the door often tell you, " We
have seen better days ;" but the Christian
is one whose best days are " not seen as
yet." Eye hath not seen what God has

prepared for his people ; and amid all your toils and privations will it not cheer you to think, " My better days are coming ?"

And would it not be delightful to have always a good employer ? Some have masters and mistresses whom there is no pleasure in serving. They are stiff and cold, and they feel no interest in you. Or they are coarse and bitter ; they give their orders with a threat, and reward you with a frown. Or they are mean and suspicious ; accusing you when innocent, and condemning you unheard. And you grudge to waste your strength on thankless toil. It hurts you to be treated like a felon or a foe; and you know not which is hardest—to be blamed when you have done no wrong, or to win no notice and no thanks when you have done your very best. But you must learn to look higher. Enter the service of the Lord Jesus, and whatsoever you do you will then " do heartily, as unto the Lord, and not unto men." Without leaving your present place you will then have

a Master wise, and kind, and worthy of
your utmost efforts ; and for his sake you
will be " subject, not only to the good and
gentle, but also to the froward." And so
long as they ask you to do nothing sinful,
whatever your earthly superiors enjoin, you
will do it thoroughly and cheerfully, for the
sake of your Master in heaven. As you
pursue your lonely task, and ply your weary
toil, you will hear his own voice saying,
" Occupy till I come ;" and the thought
that he has put you there will convert the
meanest station into a post of honor. Even
trials you will hail as that discipline which
his wisdom prescribes ; and when nothing
else could keep up your courage, it will be
enough to think of the day when — forgiving all their faults, and only remembering
their labors of love — he will say to every
meek and persevering disciple, " Well done,
good and faithful servant, enter into the joy
of thy Lord."

Besides, if you become the servant of
the Lord Jesus, you will have an Almighty

Friend to whom to go in all your fears and
sorrows. One of your trials is your loneliness. You have no affectionate counsel-
lor now like what you had at home ; and
you would be thankful for some one who
would take a kind interest in your welfare — who would listen to your griefs —
and who would help you to do what is
right, and shun what is wrong. For that
purpose, there is no friend like the Saviour;
none so wise, so powerful, so holy; and,
what makes him the very one you need, he
is a Friend constantly at hand. You do
not see him, but he is ever present, and
will hear you if you pray. Tell him of
your sins and temptations, and he will help
you to overcome them. Tell him of your
troubles, and he will comfort you. Tell
him of your difficulties, and perhaps, while
you are yet speaking, they will vanish and
disappear. And though you may not have
much opportunity for prayer, the Lord is
very pitiful ; and just as he heard Nehe-
miah with the king's wine-cup in his

hand, and answered the prayer which
Eliezer offered as he knelt beside his master's camel, so, if you are really earnest,
the Lord will hear the petition which you
breathe to him at any time and in any
place. I lately read of a servant, in Scotland, who could get no retirement in the
house, but she used to pray silently as she
went to the well for water; "and often,"
she said, "as I stood beside the well,
the same condescending Redeemer who
manifested himself to the poor woman at
Jacob's well, revealed himself to me."
And do you take for the guide of your
youth that Saviour, as merciful as he is
almighty, and then you can never be friend-
less or forlorn. To all your cares and sorrows his ear will be ever open; and, while
no danger nor distress can escape his watch-
ful eye, through every stage of life and in
every scene of action, he will graciously
uphold you by the Holy Spirit's comfort
and control.

Dear reader, will you not, from this time

onward, love and serve this Saviour? Will
you not go to him, and beg that he would
receive a poor, unworthy sinner, who has
heard of his kindness, and who nopes in
his mercy? Will you not intrust to him
the keeping of your soul, and the care of
all your interests? And as he most willingly receives you, so will not you humbly
and diligently follow him? And are you
not saying already, " Lord, what wouldst
thou have me to do?—Speak, Lord, for
thy servant heareth?"

Yes, and to you the Lord hath spoken.
He who gave the Bible, had a great care
for servants; and to copy all the passages
especially suited to you would fill this paper. I hope you will search them out,
and mark them when you find them, and
read them often over. In the meanwhile,
as a specimen, here are three. Listen to
the voice of Jesus, and let the holy accents
sink into your inmost soul:—

" Servants, obey in all things your masters according to the flesh; not with eye-

service, as men-pleasers; but in singleness of heart, fearing God: and whatsoever ye do, do it heartily, as to the Lord, and not unto men; knowing that of the Lord ye shall receive the reward of the inheritance : for ye serve the Lord Christ. But he that doeth wrong shall receive for the wrong which he hath done: and there is no respect of persons."*

"Exhort servants to be obedient unto their own masters, and to please them well in all things; not answering again: not purloining, but showing all good fidelity; that they may adorn the doctrine of God our Saviour in all things. For the grace of God that bringeth salvation hath appeared to all men, teaching us that, denying ungodliness and worldly lusts, we should live soberly, righteously, and godly, in this present world; looking for that blessed hope, and the glorious appearing of the great God and our Saviour Jesus Christ; who gave himself for us, that he might

* Colossians, iii. 22–25.

redeem us from all iniquity, and purify unto himself a peculiar people, zealous of good works."*

"Servants, be subject to your masters with all fear; not only to the good and gentle, but also to the froward. For this is thankworthy, if a man for conscience toward God endure grief, suffering wrongfully. For what glory is it, if, when ye be buffeted for your faults, ye shall take it patiently? but if, when ye do well, and suffer for it, ye take it patiently, this is acceptable with God. For even hereunto were ye called: because Christ also suffered for us, leaving us an example, that ye should follow his steps: who did no sin, neither was guile found in his mouth: who, when he was reviled, reviled not again; when he suffered, he threatened not; but committed himself to him that judgeth righteously: who his ownself bare our sins in his own body on the tree, that we, being dead to sins, should live unto righteous-

* Titus, ii. 9–14.

ness: by whose stripes ye were healed. For ye were as sheep going astray; but are now returned unto the Shepherd and Bishop of your souls."*

From these passages, you see that your first duty is obedience. Of course, you must not tell lies, nor do anything wicked, to please your employer; but so long as you remain in his service, and so long as his commands do not contradict the commands of God, you must do whatever he bids you. And do it cheerfully: even if you would rather be doing something else, still "do it heartily; do it as to the Lord, and not unto men." The beauty of obedience is its frankness. There was a youth to whom his father said, "Go work in my vineyard to-day:" but he answered, crossly, "I will not." It was not that he was particularly lazy, nor that he had no love to his father; for, on thinking better about it, he laid off his coat and took up his tools, and when his father stepped into the vine

* 1 Peter ii. 18—25.

yard by-and-by, the lad was at work like a
hero.   But it was a great pity, that churl-
ish answer; it left a pang in his parent's
heart, and it was not till he had made it up
with his father, that he felt quite right in
his own.   And if you would do your work
with comfort, do it cheerfully, and do it instantly.   Never " answer again;" and let
it never be seen, by your sour or lowering
countenance, that you are vexed at any
order.   The way to make it easy is to take
it heartily; and the way to make masters and
mistresses kind and considerate, is for servants to be cordial at their work, and cheerful in their compliance.   But a very foolish
plan is first to sulk, and then to obey: it
loses time, it loses credit, and it loses good
situations.

We can scarcely lay too much stress
upon temper; for few tempers are naturally
good, and yours is exposed to many trials.
Sometimes you are called away in the
midst of your work, and the labor of an
hour is lost.   Or you are ordered to attend

to some matter which does not belong to
your department; or fellow-servants play
tricks on you, and, instead of helping you,
increase your trouble ; or you are obliged
to sit up late and rise early, and, out of
sorts and out of spirits, you grow morose
and miserable. And it must be confessed
that this is trying to flesh and blood ; but,
just on account of these trials, you are the
more bound to pray for a meek and quiet
spirit. To its possessor it is not only an
" ornament,"* but an unspeakable comfort.
Even where no sharp answer is given, people do not like to hear doors slamming,
and porcelain smashing, and fire-irons rat
tling, and other signs of the tempest down
stairs ; but be they " froward" themselves,
or be they good and gentle, they like to see
their attendants calm and courteous. They
like that their door should be opened to
their friends, by one who wears a welcome
in her smiling faee, and they feel it a personal compliment when every office is per-

* 1 Petei iii. 4.

formed with mild alacrity and evident good will. Even though they may not like your piety, they will prize your politeness, and by your civil and respectful demeanor, you will adorn the religion you profess. And you will smooth your daily path, and perform life's journey more pleasantly. You have looked at a country cart; and when there was need of haste, it was a clumsy sight to see it lurching and hobbling along the road, and a harsh tune to listen to its screeching axle and jangling gear, till some projecting stone capsized it, and it spread from ditch to dike, a wreck of splintered deals and broken spars. And along the same road you have seen the chariot speeding, and as on liquid axle and jaunty springs it skimmed the track, and courtesied over the clods and the stones, its flight was silent and steady, as if wings opened and shut from every wheel. So is it painful to see a fitful temper jolting and jarring along its rugged course, provoked at every hinderance, announcing its progress by perpetual discord, and finally upset by some little interruption, which a more elastic spirit would have lightly glided over. And a happy thing it is to see that wretched temper changed, and as it revolves through daily duties, vaulting over annoyances and stumbling-blocks, and holding on its way with neither dust nor din. Ruth Clark, whose story you would do well to read, once had a violent temper; but after the grace of God had reached her, she began to watch and pray against this proud spirit, and so entirely was it subdued, that " persons living constantly with her would never have suspected that she had formerly been its slave." And, however unruly your spirit at present is, if you strive constantly against it, and cry for help to the Lamb of God, he will give you the victory, and bless you with a spirit like his own— " gentle, meek, and mild."

Whatever be the place you hold, you can not discharge its duties without good sense, as well as good health and good

principle; but if already blessed with these
mercies, there is nothing to hinder you
from becoming a first-rate servant; and,
whatever may be his calling in life, every
Christian should be first-rate in his own
department. In every calling, however, it
needs pains and perseverance to reach perfection. It was by long practice, and after
many lessons, that Sir Thomas Lawrence
became a first-rate painter; and it was by
great humility, and by taking hints from
every one, that John Dalton became a first-
rate chemist; and it is by like means that
you are to become a first rate servant. Be
humble, and then you will be thankful for
every hint. You will observe how older
and more accomplished servants do their
work, and you will try and try again, till
you can do it as well as they. And when
your mistress or a friend is kind enough to
explain any process, you will carefully
attend, and not need to be told it again.
And thus, step by step, you will get on,
till you become so neat and orderly, that,

in all your little realm of rooms and cupboards, everything will find its proper place, and wear its tidiest look; so accurate and punctual, that you will forget no messages, and will have all things ready at the minute; so dexterous and expert, that it will seem as if there were a charm in your finger-points, and as if every article you touched understood your meaning; so calm and self-possessed, that confusion will clear up, and disorder will arrange itself when you come in; so thoughtful and considerate, that you will find out employment for yourself, and attend to matters which, but for you, would be omitted: and when you have reached this degree of skill and experience, it will be no flattery to call you a first-rate servant.*

* Those who are anxious to improve will find many useful hints in "the Servants' Magazine"—a penny periodical published monthly by the "Female Aid Society." This society has done much good; and it may be useful to mention, here, that it maintains a "Servants' Home and Registry" at No. 5 Millman street, near Bedford row, where respectable female servants are

Try to do good in the place of your sojourn. When Mr. Fletcher, of Madeley, was tutor in a Shropshire family, he had some respect for religion, but not enough to make him religious. One sabbath evening, a pious servant came into his study to make up the fire, and seeing him writing music, she said, with deep concern, "Oh, sir! I am sorry to see you so employed on the Lord's day." And though very angry at the moment, after she went out, he put away the music, and never copied any more on the sabbath. I am not sure, however, that reproof is the best way of doing good to superiors. A word modestly spoken, and by a person of tried consistency,

lodged, and assisted in finding situations, at a very moderate charge.

In the same neighborhood—that is, at No. 22 New Ormond street—is a school for training servants, maintained by the Hon. Mrs. Kinnaird and her friends. A hundred girls are at present attending it, who, but for its advantages, would never have been fit for respectable service. We mention it here, partly to record the delight we have experienced in visiting it, and partly in the hope that it may suggest to some benevolent reader the establishment of similar institutions elsewhere.

may sometimes prove a word in season, but it is more likely to be resented as rudeness, and you may only irritate those whom you meant to reform. Far more effectual is the silent eloquence of a lowly, cheerful, and obliging piety; and if some have been repelled from the gospel by the preaching tone and arrogant air of servants who professed it, others have been won by the gainly demeanor of servants who adorned it. But try to do good to your fellow-servants. If you are enabled to live soberly, righteously, and godly; if they see you correct, and truthful, and devout, but if at the same time you are kind and affable, you will gain great influence over them; and by lending them books, or persuading them to come with you to the house of God, you may confer a lasting blessing on their souls. And if you have the charge of children, teach them texts and hymns, and speak to them affectionately about the Saviour, and tell them Bible stories, and warn them with solemn tenderness against lying, and pride, and quarrelling, and selfishness, and the other sins of childhood.

A young girl once went to a thoughtless family in the north of Ireland. She loved her Bible, but the young ladies on whom she waited laughed at her religion. She tried all she could to be attentive and useful to them ; and to please her they sometimes let her read aloud a chapter when they had gone to bed. But by-and-by a dangerous sickness seized her. It was a fever, and her young friends were not allowed to see her, but they heard how happy she was amidst all her sufferings. And after she had gone to Jesus, the two oldest remembered what she used to say while yet with them, and began to **read** the Bible for themselves, till they found peace in the same Saviour, and till at last religion spread through this once careless family. Happy maid! when she meets on high the endeared objects of her prayers, and this unhoped result of her gentle piety.

Will you permit me to add that few classes in modern society are so rich as domestic servants? You have no rent, no rates to pay; you need buy neither coals nor candles, nor food, nor (clothing excepted) any of those endless commodities which daily tax the householder; and, though your income is small, you yourself are rich, for you might easily save the half of it. Sad pity that so many squander on treats or useless trinkets the wages for which they work so hard! Would it not be nobler to do as some have done, and educate a nephew, or young brother? or do as others have done, and maintain in comfort an infirm or aged parent? And would it not be wiser to lay up a good foundation against the coming time, and, by putting aside a monthly or yearly sum, to build a bulwark between yourself and future poverty? That shilling which you spent at the pastry-cook's would have bought a Bible for a heathen family. That crown which you lavished on the brooch or the bracelet would have

bought a blanket for your poor old grand-
father, and many a time would his palsied
limbs have thanked you during these bitter
nights. And those sovereigns and tens of
pounds which have melted away, you know
not how, had the bank or the benefit fund*
received them, with what a lightened look
might you now survey those hapless years
when you shall be able to work or earn no
longer! What think you? Will you
henceforth try the plan of frugality and self-

* There is such a fund connected with the Servants'
Benevolent Institution, 32 Sackville street. Servants
sometimes lend money to relatives commencing business,
or to persons who offer them a tempting interest. Now,
a tempting interest just means a terrible risk. It means
that the borrower is so unlikely ever to return the loan,
that people whose business it is to lend money can not
trust them; and therefore he is obliged to offer six and
eight per cent. to servants, and widowed ladies, and
people who know nothing of business, and are likely to
take the bait. In regard to relations: it may often be
kind and helpful to give them a present of money, but
a loan is neither kind nor helpful. It is not kind, for
you give it with the hope of getting it all again; and it
is not helpful, for "easily gotten quickly goes;" and at
the end of the year they will need it as much as ever.
In *giving*, you only hope for gratitude, and are pretty
sure to get it: in *lending*, people hope for both gratitude and repayment, and usually get neither.

denial? Will you try how little may suffice
for your present self, and how much you
can save for your aged and worn-out self?
and how much you can spare for those dear
ones who do not fare so well nor lodge so
pleasantly as you? Will you just count up
how much you have expended on the " lust
of the eye, and the pride of life ?" on dress,
and vanity, and idle show ? These fancies
did you no service at the time, and they
all have perished in the using. Be persuaded, how, to try the more excellent
plan ; and though you may find it hard at
first to pass bright ribands and silken bar-
gains, there is a threefold pleasure which
will soon requite you: the sweetness of
self-denial, the comfort of having somewhat
provided against evil days, and the luxury
of doing good.

But you say that I have quite mistaken
in supposing you unhappy in your present
place. The family in which Providence
has cast your lot is kind and considerate.
It is a family in which God is feared and

worshipped, and you are encouraged to frequent his house, and sanctify his sabbath. If so, determine that no whim nor misconduct of yours shall ever part you from God's people. Put forth your utmost efforts to win their confidence, and let cheerful industry be your daily thank-offering to Him who has so highly favored you. And, though a Christian servant will not waste her master's property, whosoever that master be, it is a great comfort when you think that the food or fuel which you save, or the furniture of which you are so careful, is something husbanded for the poor, or for the Christian treasury. And, though a Christian servant will be active, and obliging, and orderly, whatever her employers are, she has another motive added, when she thinks that her civility, and neatness, and good sense, are increasing the happiness of a Christian home. Melancthon, the great reformer, was not rich, but he loved to show hospitality, and he needed to buy books, and travel a great deal in the service of the

church, and he often said that he owed it all
to the good management of his old and
faithful servant, John of Sweden. And
just as we have known pious servants, who,
rather than leave a pious family, would have
continued to serve for nothing, so we have
also known Christian families who, rather
than see a faithful servant homeless in her
declining days, were glad to retain, as an
old friend, the inmate whom they had first
received beneath their roof as a servant—
" not now a servant, but a mother, a sister,
beloved in the Lord."

25

THE TRUE DISCIPLE.

This concluding paper the author respectfully inscribes to his more thoughtful readers. He has been frequently told that his essays are above the comprehension of "working people;" but that complaint has seldom come from themselves. Among hard-workers there are many hard-thinkers, and there are thousands whose capacity and education are at least equal to anything contained in the foregoing pages. With an eye to that honorable class, the readers and the thinkers among his industrious fellow-citizens, the author has written most of the bygone numbers; and if some of the following paragraphs are not so plain as they ought to be, he would humbly beg for them the benefit of a second perusal.—November 27, 1848

EVER since the world sinned and woke up to misery, there is one absentee whom all have agreed in deploring. Every age has asked tidings of her from the age that went before, and from the one which came after; and even the most indolent have put forth an effort, and have joined their neighbors in searching for this fugitive. Some

THE TRUE DISCIPLE.

have dived into the billowy main, and sought
her in pearly grottoes and coral caves. And
some have bored into the solid rock, and
rummaged for her in the mountain roots.
And some have risen to where the eagles
poise, and have scanned in successive hori-
zons the habitable surface; but all have
got the same report. "Where is happiness?"—"Not in me," cries the leafy
grove; "nor in me," booms the sounding
tide; "nor in me," rumbles gaunt and hollow from the dusky mine. And failing to
detect her in life's by-paths and open ways,
her votaries have reared decoys or shrines
into which she haply might turn aside.
But all of them have failed entirely. Thea-
tres, dancing-saloons, gin-palaces, racing-
booths—there is no authentic instance that
she ever entered one of them. And though
some have fancied that they glimpsed her
—"yes, yes," they whisper, "yonder she
passed; and in that hall of science, in that
temple of knowledge, in that sweet home,
you'll find her;" by the time you reached

it, there was a death's-head at the door,
and a " Mene Tekel" on the wall. " Not
in me," sighed vain philosophy ; and " not
in me," re-echoed the worldling's rifled
home.

But where .s happiness? Man knows
that she is not dead but disappeared ; and
ever since under the forbidden tree he ate
the bitter-sweet and startled her away, he
has longed to find that other and enlighten-
ing fruit which would reveal her to his eyes
again. And this is the boon which the
world's teachers have undertaken to supply.
They have come from time to time, seers
and sages, Thales, Pythagoras, Zoroaster,
Epicurus, Con-fu-tze, and to humanity's
wondering gaze they have held up apples,
us they said, fresh gathered from the Tree
of Life. But after rushing and jostling
round them, and getting at great cost a prize,
these all proved naught to the hungry buy-
er. The golden apples were mere make-
believes ; hollow rinds, painted shells filled
up with trash or trifles. Some ate, and still

their soul had appetite; others ate, and were poisoned.

At last, along the path which a hundred prophecies had carved and smoothed, "the desire of all nations"—the Son of God—appeared. And from the paradise above he fetched the long-lost secret. Himself "the truth;" his every sentence freighted with majesty, and fragrant with heaven's sanctity; it needed not the frequent miracle to compel the exclamation, "Rabbi, we know that thou art a teacher come from God." He did not reason; he revealed. His sayings were not the conjectures of keen sagacity, nor even the recollections of an angel visiter; but they were authoritative words—the insight of Omniscience, the oracle of incarnate Deity. And giving freely to all comers "the apples of gold" from his "basket of silver," the dim and the famished ate, and with open eyes looking up, in himself they recognised the answer to the ancient query. "What is happiness?"—"Come unto me," is the Saviour's reply; " come unto me, all ye that labor and are heavy laden, and I will give you rest. Take my yoke upon you, and learn of me; for I am meek and lowly in heart: and ye shall find rest unto your souls."—" Where is happiness?" Here, at the feet of Immanuel. And then, and since, thousands have verified the saying. In the words of Jesus they have discovered the boon for which their understandings longed—conclusive and soul-filling knowl-edge; and in his person and work they have found the good for which their conscience craved—a saving and sanctifying Power.

To the great question, What is happi-ness? Jesus is the embodied answer— at once the teacher and the lesson. The question had been asked for ages, and some hundred solutions had been proposed. And in the outset of his ministry the Saviour took it up, and gave the final answer. What is happiness? " Happy are the humble. Happy are the contrite. Happy are the meek. Happy are they who hunger after righteousness. Happy are the merciful, the pure in heart, the peace-makers, the men persecuted for righteousness."* In

* The reader could not do better than go carefully over the Sermon on the Mount. He will find it in the fifth, sixth, and seventh chapters of Matthew. We have known of repeated instances where persons received their first prepossession for Christianity from that matchless effusion of incarnate goodness. The following passage occurs in Sir James Mackintosh's Indian Journal : " I have just glanced over Jeremy Taylor on the Beatitudes. The selection is made in the most sublime spirit of virtue. Of their transcendent excellence I can find no words to express my admiration and reverence. ' Blessed are the merciful, for they shall obtain mercy.'—' Put on, my beloved, *as the elect of God*, bowels of mercy.' At last the divine speaker rises to the summit of moral sublimity. ' Blessed are they who are persecuted for righteousness' sake.' For a moment, O teacher blessed, I taste the unspeakable delight of feeling myself to be better. I feel, as in the days of my youth, that hunger and thirst after righteousness, which long habits of infirmity, and the low concerns of the world, have contributed to extinguish."—Life ii., 125. At the moment when he wrote these words, we fear that this fine intellect was skeptical. It was far otherwise at last. His daughter says, telling of his latter hours, " I said to him, ' Jesus Christ loves you ;' he answered slowly, and, pausing between each word, ' Jesus Christ—love—the same thing.' He uttered these last words with a most sweet smile. After a long silence he said, ' I believe—.' We said, in a voice of inquiry, ' in God ?' He answered, ' in Jesus.' He spoke but once more after this. Upon our inquiry how he felt, he said he was ' happy.' "

other words, he declared that happiness is goodness. A holy nature is a happy one. But was not that a blank and confounding announcement? To tell the wicked people all around him — the fierce, and quarrelsome, and licentious spirits who thronged the mountain side, " Blessed are the merciful, the pure, the peaceful;" was not that to lay a gravestone on their hopes? Was it not saying to his auditors, " Happiness is goodness, and so it never can be yours?" And had the teaching of Jesus ended there, he would have left mankind in gloomy possession of a glorious truth ; he would have left it a wiser but a sadder world. But in the minds of such as felt themselves guilty and unholy, that announcement raised two other questions. Will God pardon the past? And if he should, how are we to get those holy dispositions which are so essential to blessedness? And at sundry times, and in divers places, he answered both these questions. " Will God pardon the past?" —" Yes; for God so

loved the world, that he gave his only begotten Son, that whosoever believeth in him
should not perish, but have everlasting life."
That is, "accept my atonement, and you
shall not die for your own sin. Employ
me as your Mediator, and eternal life is
your own. Believe and be forgiven."
Again. "Supposing sin is pardoned, how
are holy dispositions to be created and fos-
tered in this wicked heart of mine?"——
"Jesus stood and cried, If any man thirst
(for holiness) let him come unto me, and
drink. He that believeth on me, out of his
heart shall flow rivers of living water. This
spake he of the Spirit, which they that believe on him should receive." That is,
"Come to me as disciples, and be filled
with the Holy Ghost. Believe on me, and
find pure water welling through your nature's bitter soil. Believe, and be filled
with holy desires and dispositions." So
that, in its entireness, Christ's doctrine came
to this—"A new and holy nature is blessedness. Believe in me, and your nature

will be new and holy, and you yourself be blessed."

We have said that Christ was not only the great Teacher, but the great Lesson. Perhaps this will be plainer if we take another grand question. The world asks, What is happiness? But that can only be answered by meeting another inquiry — What is God? Is he just, and good, and true? And how is he disposed toward sinners of our race? Is he placable? Is he propitious? Or is he stern and vindictive, and determined to destroy us? Or is he altogether indifferent to our weal or wo? Among thoughtful men these queries had been often mooted, and doubtless the first disciples of Jesus had often mused and pondered over them; and at last, when he was about to leave them, one put the question express. The Master had told them that the time was come, and that he must now return to the Father; and feeling that the opportunity must not be lost, Philip exclaimed, "Lord, show us the

Father, and it sufficeth us." "That is the very thing for which our hearts are breaking: we know not the living God. Show us the Father, and fill the great gap in our knowledge—the mighty chasm in our comfort." And Jesus answered, "Have I been so long time with you, and yet hast thou not known me, Philip? HE THAT HATH SEEN ME, HATH SEEN THE FATHER." As much as if he had said, "Our nature is identical; our will is one. All that you need ever know of God is manifest in me. You wonder if God is holy, and just, and true: have you not seen me? You wonder if God is kind, and good, and loving: have I been so long time with you, and yet have you not known me? You wonder if God be gracious and ready to forgive: did I scruple in receiving you?" And so, my dear friends, it is life eternal to know the only true God: and you will know him if you know Jesus, whom he has sent. The Son is the express image of the Father, and if you would have confidence toward

God, you must take the Lord Jesus as
your theology. Do not think that the
Father is less compassionate, less condescending, less forgiving, than the Son.
Do not think of him as less mindful of
you, or less loving. Do not think of him
as less willing for your salvation than the
Redeemer who died on Calvary; or less
ready to hear and answer prayer than that
Intercessor in whose name your prayers
ascend. He that hath seen the Son hath
seen the Father; and if you would escape
false terror, and ignorant surmisings, and
idolatrous illusions, think of Jesus when
you think of God.

In order to be truly happy, you must
have some sufficient end in living. And
this, again, has moved much controversy.
What is the object to which an immortal
nature may devote itself most worthily?
Which is the highest good? And some
have answered, TRUTH. They have con-
secrated their days and nights to learning,
and have lived and labored for the true.

And others have maintained that the very crown of excellence is BEAUTY; and in painting, or verse, or music, they have yearned and struggled toward their fair and ever-soaring ideal. And others averring that GOODNESS is the truest joy — that moral rectitude is the topmost apex and converging goal to which all intelligence should tend and travel — they have resolved to spend and be spent for this, and have lived and died the devotees of virtue. But if you, my friends, understand the gospel, you have found the true philosophy; if you know Christ, you have learned the SUPREME FELICITY. In the Alpha and Omega — in the all-inclusive Excellence — in Immanuel, you possess at once the good, the true, the beautiful: the good, for he is the Holy One of God ;—the true, for he is the Amen—the truth-speaking and truth-im bodying I Am ;—the beautiful, for—himself the perfection of beauty — to one vision of his infinite mind his Omnipotence said, " Let it be," and in this fair universe you

24

behold the result. Yes, it is a blessed thing to have a life rightly directed and worthily bestowed; not to live for a phantom, but for something real; not to live for something insufficient or subordinate, but for a high and glorious end; not to live for something alien or irrelevant, but for an object which claims and can requite your service. Live to Christ, and then you live to highest purpose. Live to Christ, and then you live to him who loved you, and gave himself for you. Live to Christ, and then you have a patron, beneath whose smile you may dive into the deepest truth, and soar into the highest beauty. Live to Christ, and then you have an Almighty Friend, into whose arms you may consign your worldly calling and your dearest friends; and, after he has "put his hands upon them and blessed them," may receive them back, no longer stolen joys, but hallowed loans, and mercies bright with a Redeemer's benison. Live to Christ, and then your soul is joined to that fountain of unfailing strength, which gives at once the zest and power of goodness. If you would serve your family, your country, your friends, live to Jesus Christ. If you would have your existence raised to its highest level, and your faculties drawn forth to their fullest exercise, with you let it "to live" be "Christ." And if you would begin betimes that devout and benignant life which Heaven prolongs and perfects, learn from Jesus how to live.

For it is in the living Saviour that we must learn the great life-lesson. Jesus was divine, but he was also human. He dwelt among us not only to show us what God is, but what we should be. He left to his people an example that they should follow his steps; and the best idea of a Christian is "one in whom the life of Jesus is once more manifest." We greatly needed such a pattern. We did not want so much one who should give us new rules and directions how to live, as one who should himself be a noble specimen. And Jesus was that specimen. In books, and especially in the inspired writings, holy character had been minutely described, and the rule of conduct had been carefully laid down. But what others taught, Jesus did and Jesus was. Before his appearing, too, there had been some splendid instances of isolated excellence — virtues blazing, by ones and twos, from dark and defective natures ; but reabsorbing into his illustrious excellence all these scattered beams, the character of Jesus exhibited no defect nor dimness. Without a spot he shone, the Sun of Righteousness — without eclipse or obscuration, " the Light of the world" — a living Decalogue, where each command was inscribed in letters of brightness on tablets of love.

Behold him — how devout. There was one thing which made the Man of sorrows still the Man of joys. He could not lose the sense of the Father's love. There spread constantly round him that melodious baptism which first issued from the excel-

lent glory, " This is my beloved Son, in
whom I am well pleased." In the strength
of this assurance, he journeyed day by
day, and found it meat and drink to do his
Father's will. And when the toilsome
day was done, and he pensively eyed the
fox leaving his lair and the bird wending
home to her eyry, though his worn body
knew no couch, his happy spirit sought
its home in the bosom of its God. The
Father loved him, and that love was the
rod and staff of pilgrim Messiah. It led
him in the paths of righteousness, and
comforted him in the valley of death-
shadow; and as soon as in his darkest
night he waved its transforming wand,
Gethsemane lit up green pasture, and
Kedron spread out still water.

And so, dear reader, do you enter into
the Saviour's joy. In becoming his disciple, he says, " My peace I give unto you."
That same peace which was his constant
portion here below, he bought for sinners
with his blood. And nothing can you do

24*

to the Redeemer more joyful, and to the
Father more glorifying, and to your own
soul more hallowing, that when in the surety's name you claim the peace of God.
Love Jesus, and the Father himself will
love you ; and instead of skulking through
life a culprit or a convict, " accepted in the
Beloved," you may lift up the eye of a
dear and trustful child.   If you would have
your affections fixed to God, the cord of
his own love must fasten them.   If you
would be strong for work or trial, the joy
of the Lord must be your strength.   If
you would possess a deep and genuine holiness, the very God of peace must be your
sanctifier.   And if, when times are dark —
when the world looks gloomy, or shadows
from the sepulchre are creeping round you
—if you would still have brightness on
your onward path, learn to look up to God
in Christ as your own God for ever and for
ever.

And   see him—so pure of purpose
Placed before you is a casket of gold, and

you are asked to guess what it contains;
and looking at its exquisite tracery and
costly material, you think of a blazing diamond or a monarch's signet-ring. Guess?
You can not guess. They open it, and reveal a spider, a scorpion, or a spinning-
worm! And surveying a human soul, you
view the finest casket in this world. Made
on a heavenly pattern, with powers so ca-
pacious, and feelings so susceptible, in order to be worthily occupied, it would need
to be filled with some lofty purpose, some
pure and noble motive. My reader, you
have got that casket. What have you put
in it? What is the thing which chiefly
occupies your thoughts? Your great pursuit and pleasure? What impels you to
exertion? Is it money? Is it popularity
and praise? Is it dress? Is it dainty
food? Is it some fierce and evil passion?
Is it envy? Is it resentment? Is it selfishness? Is it the wish to achieve your own
personal ease and comfort? Is it something
so paltry that you are ashamed to call it the

business of life?—something so baleful
that it degrades and destroys the heart which
hides it? Viewed in his world-ward aspect, the Saviour's one motive was philanthropy. His life-long business was to do
good to the bodies and the souls of those
around him. To pluck brands from the
burning, to instruct the ignorant, to reclaim
the vicious, to restore the fallen, to convert
the soul, to lighten the burden of wo, to
heal disease, to banish misery, to bind up
the broken heart—this was his daily calling, this was his continuous pursuit. "I
must do cures to-day and to-morrow, and
the third day I shall be glorified." Nico-
demus did not come so late but that he was
glad to see him, and the Samaritan woman
did not find him so exhausted, but the hope
of saving her soul made him forgetful of
fatigue. And so pure was this passion, so
irrespective of accidental circumstances, or
of the present attractiveness of its objects, that
the leper and the lunatic, the blind beggar
and the howling demoniac, Malchus in the

act of arresting him, and the very men who
slew him, all came in for an ungrudging
share. His last prayer was intercession;
his last business was beneficence. " Father,
forgive them ;"—" Woman, behold thy
son ; Disciple, behold thy mother ;" and
having prayed for his murderers and provided for Mary a home, from the contiguous
cross he bore with him to Paradise, as love's
last trophy, the spirit of the ransomed thief.

Reader, let the mind be in you which
was in Christ Jesus. Seek to have your
bosom filled with pure kindness and holy
compassion—a compassion various as is
human sorrow—a kindness which shall
still be flowing while life itself is ebbing.
Cease to be selfish. Learn the blessedness
of doing good. Even you can contribute
to that great work—the making of a bad
world better. Is there no acquaintance over
whom you have influence? None whom
you might reclaim from a bad habit? None
whom you might induce to read some useful book, or attend the house of God? Are

there no poor children whom you might collect on a sabbath afternoon, and teach them a Bible lesson? Is there no sick neighbor to whom you might carry a little comfort—something nice to tempt his listless palate? No invalid friend whom you might cheer with an hour of your company, or to whom you might read or say something for the good of his soul? At all events, you can be doing good at home. You can minister to the wants of some aged parent. You can sooth the grief of some bereaved relation. You can lend a helping hand, and lighten their labors who have got too much to do. With a firm but fatherly control, you can guide your children in wisdom's ways. And you can diffuse throughout your dwelling that sweetest music—cheerful and approving words; that brightest light—the clear shining of a cordial countenance. And when God in his Providence sends favorable opportunities, with self-denied and prayerful affection, you may be the means of stamping on some immortal

mind a truth or lesson as enduring as that
mind itself.

Then, too, observe how simple and how
genuine was his character! how free from
extremeness or reserve! "The Son of
man came eating and drinking." He wore
the common dress of the country. He
spoke the common language. So far as
they were innocent, he fell in with all the
common usages of the people around him.
And some were annoyed at this. They
wished that he would make himself singular. They would have liked him to keep
more aloof. Like his predecessor, John
the Baptist, they would have preferred that
he had dwelt in the desert, and fasted, and
worn a hairy mantle or some peculiar garb.
They could have wished to see him issue
on the world from some dim cloister, and
in stately speech give forth his mystic oracle, and once more vanish from the view.
But they fancied that they knew all about
him—his birthplace, his parentage, his
habits; and so long as he lived this open

and explicit life they could not surround
him with an odor of sanctity. They were
too gross to perceive how much of Heaven
he carried into Cana's feast, and with what
a god-like purpose he went to be the guest
of Matthew or Zaccheus. They forgot how
much nobler is the piety which hallows
common life, than the demureness which
flies away from it. And they did not know
that he was doing all this on purpose. He
meant his example to be a pattern to common people, and therefore he frequented
the ordinary resorts, and lived the familiar
life of men. But though he might now be
seen in the market-place or under the tem-
ple-piazza, surrounded with people from
the shops and stalls; and though you might
this afternoon meet him amidst lawyers and
courtiers, in the house of Simon the Phar-
isee; and though you might overtake him
next morning seated under a wayside tree,
and discoursing freely to his peasant-follow
ers; and though on all these occasions there
was no assumption, no reserve, no artifice,

there was, at the same time, no weakness,
no sanction to vice or folly. There was all
the refinement of a most delicate benevo-
lence, and all the majesty of a nature separate from sin. His every movement was
innocence; his every utterance was purity.
His character was like the sunbeam, visiting without degradation the poorest hovel,
and contracting no stain from the evils which
it failed to extinguish.

Reader, you are living in that world in
which the Lord Jesus chose for a season
to reside. If your piety be sound and
strong enough, common life will not make
you carnal. Have grace in your heart.
Live under the eye of God. Live in the
name of Jesus. Take your Master for
your model. Pray and labor to be in the
world as its sinless Visiter was. And if
God should give you the spirit of true dis-
cipleship, there will be a beautiful complete-
ness in your character. You will not need
to study your appearance, nor to be nervous
about people's opinions; for by its self-

25

sustaining sincerity, your conduct will sooner or later achieve its own vindication, and in her child shall Wisdom be justified. In your common talk there will be no scurrility nor scandal ; nothing false, nothing unseemly, nothing base nor vile. In your ordinary acting, there will be no crooks nor crotchets ; nothing shabby or unfair ; nothing cruel or oppressive ; nothing for which conscience can not render a good reason. But those who knelt with you at family prayer will recognise the same man when they meet you in the mart or the work-room ; and those who last saw you in the festive circle will not be startled when they find themselves beside you at the communion-table.

—

If this sketch be plain enough, you will perceive that it is to three things that the mission of Jesus Christ owes its main importance :—

He is the manifestation of God.

He is the Mediator between God and man.

And he is the model to his redeemed and regenerate people.

He is God manifest. No man hath seen the Father but the Son, and he to whom the Son hath revealed him. He that hath seen Jesus hath seen the Father. He is the express image of the Father; and as embodying all the perfections and dispositions of the invisible Godhead, Jesus is to our race the one theology.

He is also Mediator. His cross is the meeting-place betwixt God and the sinner. His blood is the sacrifice which makes it a righteous thing in God to cancel guilt, and receive the returning transgressor. His gospel is the white flag, the truce-proclaiming banner, which announces Jehovah's amnesty, and says to every rebel, Be reconciled to a reconciling God. His merit is the censer which perfumes the sinner's prayer, and makes it prevalent with a holy God. His intercession is that secret influ ence within the veil, which secures for his Church and its believing members the gift of the Holy Ghost. His love is the balm of life; his presence the antidote of death; his glory, seen and shared, the joy of heaven. So that, as the source and consummation of all our greatest blessings, Jesus is the Supreme Felicity.

And he is the pattern of his believing people. All that was human in his earthly walk is for our example, that we should follow his steps. And with such a transforming agent promised as is the Holy Ghost, and with such a pattern propounded as the perfect Saviour, there is no limit to the excellence, inward and outward, after which the followers of Jesus should aspire. To be "like him" is the privilege of a perfect world; — but how gloriously near to that likeness even now his loving people may attain, the Bible nowhere limits. But the believer, whose character is strong without hardness, and gentle without weakness — who is consumed with the

zeal of God, and who still glows with good
will to man—who is spiritual but not sanc-
timonious, diligent and withal devout, vigorous in action and patient in endurance,—
that consistent disciple bears the visible
lineaments of the Elder Brother. And as
supplying our world with the first and only
instance of excellence fully developed and
perfectly proportioned—goodness in its
entireness, and each grace in its inten-
sity—the life of Jesus is the great text-
book of ethics—the grand lesson in practical piety.

You also perceive that Christianity, or
the knowledge of Christ, is "the most excellent of all the sciences." Some knowledge
is entertaining, and some is useful; but this
knowledge is essential. Without it you
can not gain peace of conscience, nor that
refinement and elevation of character which
itself is happiness; and without it you can
not secure a blissful immortality. And of
all the sciences which treat the great question of human happiness, this alone is solid;

25*

for this alone is constructed from facts and confirmed by experience. Some theories are popular from age to age, but they are human compilations, and, like snow-statues reared in spring, the influence is already working which will melt them again. And other theories gleam before the fancy passing fair, and as they can not be caught, they can neither be confuted nor confirmed. Like the aurora, they flicker and amuse, but they can not be employed for practical purposes; you can not collect and retain them to light your chamber or your streets. But Christianity is as practical as it is sublime; and while it has truths which surpass the loftiest intellect, it has applications which suit the lowliest purposes. And it has a distinction peculiar to itself, one which should recommend it now, even as it will endear it on a dying day; it is the only REVELATION. God was in it at the first—God is in it still. Hearkening to other teachers, you may learn truth and falsehood ogether; but sitting at the feet of Jesus, you can learn no error there. Listening to his words, you hear the voice of God, and nothing will need to be unlearned in eternity which you have once acquired from him.

In the old schools of philosophy, it was usual for the pupils to bring a present to their teacher at the commencement of each term. And on one of these occasions, when his disciples, one by one, were going up with their gifts to Socrates, a poor youth hung back, and there was something like a blush upon his cheek, and something like a tear in his eye, for silver and gold he had none. But when all the rest had gone forward and presented their offering, he flung himself at the feet of the sage, and cried, "O Socrates, I give thee myself." And this is the offering which the Lord Jesus asks of you. Give him yourself. Rise, take up the cross, and follow him. In modesty and affection, become his disciple, and he will not only make you welcome to his lessons, but he will make you a sharer

in his heavenly life. He will give you the
Holy Spirit. That divine Enlightener will
open your understanding to receive the
Saviour's doctrine, and will fill your soul
with truth's vitality. And do not despond
because of what you at present are. "This
man receiveth sinners;" and in receiving
you, he will make you a "new creature."
Arise, he calleth you. Become his disciple; and, like John, imbibing sanctity from
the bosom where he laid his listening ear —
like Thomas, lingering near his person, but
carrying in his heart a stony doubt, a stub-
born misgiving, till, in the flash of over
whelming evidence, that doubt, that mis
giving, was fused into faith and weeping
wonder — like Paul, who, in every pulse
of his intensified existence, felt the life of
Jesus throb. and who, next to the desire of
being with him, burned with ardor to be
like him, — however scanty your present
knowledge, you will learn in proportion as
you love; however many your present
doubts, they will all be drowned in adora·

tion and astonishment, while you can only cry, "My Lord, and my God!" And however defective your present character, there will be kindled in your soul a hope and an effort — the hope that when he appears, you shall be like him — the effort to purify yourself as Christ is pure.

FAREWELL, my reader. To write these papers has been a pleasant task. I have liked the thought that I was working for working men. It has carried me back to the days when the gospel was new and the Church was young; and it has more endeared that heavenly Teacher of whom it is recorded, "the common people heard him gladly." Much would I delight to visit your abode, and learn if these friendly hints have done you any good;—but life is short, and labors multiply. Most likely this is all our earthly intercourse, and, except with pen and ink, I may never be

able to say, "Peace be to this house."
But in the Father's house are many mansions.   As the Saviour's humble disciples,
may we meet in that HAPPIEST HOME!

THE END.

www.ingramcontent.com/pod-product-compliance
Lightning Source LLC
Chambersburg PA
CBHW020952030726
47496CB00005B/1473